"You Can't Stop Trying To Carve Again,"

Jennifer stated fiercely.

"I can. And there's not a blessed thing you can do about it," Frank said tersely.

"Watch me," she said, picking up the first tool she came to and slapping the handle into his hand. "Squeeze it, damn you."

His fingers curved around the instrument.

"Tighter," she demanded, her body pressed against him in a way that had him thinking of things far softer than oak, far more compelling than carving. The force of the desire spiraling through him shook him to the very core of his being.

She folded her own hand around his, adding enough pressure to secure the knife. Every muscle in Frank's body tensed at this new strain, but he refused to acknowledge the agony of the effort. He was too stubborn and proud not to accept the challenge. Nor could he bear the thought of her moving away. God help him, he wouldn't deny himself the sweet, sweet pleasure of her nearness....

Dear Reader,

April is here and spring is in the air! But if you aren't one of those lucky people who gets to spend April in Paris, you can still take that trip to romance—with Silhouette Desire!

You can fly off to San Francisco—one of *my* favorite cities!—and meet Frank Chambers, April's *Man of the Month,* in *Dream Mender* by Sherryl Woods. Or you can get into a car and trek across America with Brooke Ferguson and Pete Cooper in *Isn't It Romantic?* by Kathleen Korbel. (No, I'm not going to tell you what Pete and Brooke are doing. You have to read the book!) And if you're feeling particularly adventurous, you can battle fish, mud and flood with Dom Seeger and Alicia Bernard in Karen Leabo's delightful *Unearthly Delights.*

Of course, we all know that you don't *have* to travel to find love. Sometimes happiness is in your own backyard. In Jackie Merritt's *Boss Lady,* very desperate and very pregnant TJ Reese meets hometown hunk Marc Torelli. Tricia Everett finds that the man of her dreams is ... her husband, in Noelle Berry McCue's *Moonlight Promise.* And Caroline Nobel returns to the man who's always lit her fire in *Hometown Man* by Jo Ann Algermissen.

So, it might not be April in Paris for you—*this* year. But don't worry, it's still love—at home or away—with Silhouette Desire.

Until next month,

Lucia Macro
Senior Editor

SHERRYL WOODS

DREAM MENDER

SILHOUETTE *Desire*®

Published by Silhouette Books New York

America's Publisher of Contemporary Romance

SILHOUETTE BOOKS
300 East 42nd St., New York, N.Y. 10017

DREAM MENDER

ISBN: 0-373-05708-3

First Silhouette Books printing April 1992

Printed in the U.S.A.

SHERRYL WOODS

lives by the ocean, which, she says, provides daily inspiration for the romance in her soul. She further explains that her years as a television critic taught her about steamy plots and humor; her years as a travel editor took her to exotic locations; and her years as a crummy weekend tennis player taught her to stick with what she enjoyed most—writing. "What better way is there," Sherryl asks, "to combine all that experience than by creating romantic stories?"

For Karon Gorham,
with thanks for her insights and technical expertise,
and for sensitive burn-unit experts everywhere

One

———

Frank Chambers prowled the narrow hospital room, feeling like a foul-tempered bear awakening from hibernation with a thorn in its paw. He stared at his own bandaged hands and muttered an oath that would have curled his mother's hair and earned him a sharp rap across his already-injured knuckles. He wanted to smash something, but settled for violently kicking a chair halfway across the hospital room. It skidded into the pale blue wall with a satisfying crash, but did nothing to improve his overall mood. His mother, a wise woman with little sympathy for self-pity, would have said it would have served him right if he'd broken his toe.

The door opened a cautious crack and yet another nurse peered in, an expression of alarm on her face. "You okay?"

"Just dandy," he growled.

When he didn't throw anything, she visibly gathered her courage and stepped inside, marching over to his bed and folding her arms across her chest, assuming a stern posture clearly meant to intimidate. Considering her tiny size, it wouldn't have been an effective stance even if he hadn't been feeling surly.

"You ought to be in bed," she announced. She pulled back the sheet and gestured in the right direction just to make her point.

He glared at her and ignored the invitation. "I ought to be at home. I'm not sick."

"That's not what your chart says."

"I don't give a—"

She never even took a breath at the interruption. She just kept on going, talking over his swearing. "Less than twenty-four hours ago you were in a serious fire. When they brought you in, you were suffering from smoke inhalation. Your blood gases still don't look all that good. You have second-degree burns on both hands. You need rest and therapy."

It was not the first time he had heard the same detailed recitation of his medical condition. "I need to go home," he repeated stubbornly. He tried another fierce scowl to emphasize the point. Grown men had cowered at that scowl. He was certain of its effectiveness.

Clearly unintimidated, the nurse rolled her eyes and left. He doubted she'd gone to get his release papers. None of the others had, either. Hell, his own mother hadn't sided with him when he'd insisted he didn't need to be admitted in the first place. He'd been whisked up to his room and hooked up to oxygen so fast it had left his head spinning. He'd tried bribing each of his brothers to spring him, but they'd ignored his pleas. Not even his softhearted baby sister had taken pity on him. She'd patted his arm and suggested to the afternoon-shift nurse that they tie him down if they had to.

"Et tu, Brute," he'd muttered as Karyn had winked at him over her shoulder. Then she'd linked arms with her new husband and sashayed off to dinner.

The attitude of the whole Chambers clan rankled. That good-natured defiance was the thanks he got for all those years when he'd put his own life on hold to help his mother raise his five brothers and his sister. When his father had died, he'd reluctantly stepped into the role of parenting and discovered that it fit, even at seventeen. Maturity and responsibility had been thrust on him, but he'd somehow liked being needed, liked being the backbone of a large and loving family. In a curious sort of way he'd even suffered through the empty-nest trauma, watching as his siblings had matured and struck off on their own.

Karyn's recent marriage to race-car driver Brad Willis might have been the first wedding in the tight-knit family, but it was hardly the first sign he'd had that it was time to get on with his own life. He'd been told to butt out so often in recent years he'd had no choice but to start focusing on himself instead of his siblings. He'd been doing just that—most of the time, anyway—until yesterday afternoon. Now, suddenly, at forty he was discovering what it was like to have the tables turned on him, to have to depend on others for his most basic needs. And, he didn't like it, not one bit. What man would? No wonder his brothers chafed at all his well-intended meddling. Now they were giving it back to him in spades.

Left alone with his unpleasant thoughts through the long night, Frank tried to face facts. He told himself he could live with the pain the doctors were warning him to expect as the nerves in his hands healed. Hell, he could even live with the long-term scars. He'd seen burn scars, and while they weren't pretty, his big, work-roughened hands hadn't been much to write home about anyway. What *was* killing him, though, what was creating this gut-wrenching fury, was the absolute, utter helplessness of it all.

He couldn't do the simplest things for himself with these layers of gauze wrapped around his fingers, turning them into fat, clumsy, useless appendages. Forget holding a fork. Forget turning on the shower or washing himself. Forget pushing a button on the damned TV remote or holding a book. He couldn't even go to the bathroom on his own. Nothing, ever, had left him feeling quite so humiliated. They might as well have lopped the damned things off at the wrist.

And all because of a stupid accident. One careless instant, a still-smoldering cigarette butt tossed into a trash barrel by one of his unthinking co-workers, and the next thing he'd known the entire woodworking shop had been in flames. He'd grabbed for a fire extinguisher, but the metal had already been a blistering red-hot temperature. He'd done the best he could, but with all the flammable material around, it had been like battling a towering inferno with a garden hose. He'd managed to get a few things out of the workroom before the blaze and smoke had gotten out of control, eventually destroying everything. He'd gone back in one last time to rescue one of his co-workers who'd panicked and found himself trapped in a workroom with no exit except through the fire. Only when he was outside, gulping oxygen and coughing his head off had he noticed the blistered, raw layers of skin on his hands. The adrenaline high had given way to shocked horror as paramedics rushed him to the hospital. His co-worker had been treated for smoke inhalation at the scene.

The injuries could have been worse, they'd told Frank in the emergency room. Third-degree burns, with the possibility of damaging tendons and bone, could have been devastating for a man who worked with his hands. His career, most likely, would have been over. He would have lost the woodworking skills that had turned his imaginative, finely crafted cabinetry into an art that was making its way into some of the finest homes in San Francisco. With second-degree injuries, he had a chance.

The recovery, though, would be slow, tedious and painful. Frank had never been out sick a day in his life. Now it appeared he was headed for a long vacation, courtesy of workmen's comp. The concept didn't sit well. Worse was the faint, terrifying possibility that he might never again be able to do the delicate, intricate carving that made his work unique and gave him such a sense of accomplishment.

By morning, after hours of focusing on the "what ifs," panic had bubbled up deep inside him. He dragged air into his injured lungs. Each breath hurt and did nothing to calm him, nothing to wipe away the bleak images of a future without the work that he loved.

Determined to get out of the hospital, even if he had to escape on his own, he used his foot to lever open the closet door. The task was easier than he'd expected, and his confidence soared. Hope crashed just as quickly with the realization that the only clothing hanging in the closet was his robe. His sooty shirt and jeans were no doubt ditched in some trash receptacle. He'd never get past the nurses' station, much less out of this place, wearing just an indecent hospital gown and a robe that still had a price tag hanging from the sleeve.

On the nightstand beside the bed the phone rang. Grateful for the interruption, Frank lunged for it, knocking it to the floor with his inept hands. Another stream of profanity turned the air blue. How the hell was he supposed to answer a phone with fingers that stuck straight out like prongs on a damned pitchfork?

"Nurse!" he bellowed, rather than bothering with the call button. "Nurse!"

He glared at the door, waiting for it to open, fuming because he couldn't even manage that simple task. This time, however, rather than inching open bit by cautious bit, the door was suddenly flung wide. Instead of a nurse, therapist Jennifer Michaels stepped into the room with all the confidence of a woman who's head hadn't yet been bitten off by the fuming, foul-tempered patient in Room 407.

Frank recognized her at once. He had still been dopey from medication when she'd poked her head into the room the previous afternoon, but he hadn't forgotten that perky, wide smile and that mop of shining Little Orphan Annie curls. Nor had he forgotten the cheerful promise that she would be back in the morning to begin his therapy.

"What do you want?" he asked, regarding her suspiciously.

Ignoring his challenging tone, she stepped briskly into the room, took in the situation at a glance and, with one graceful move, retrieved the phone from under the bed. "I was at the nurses' station when we heard your dulcet tones echoing down the hall," she told him.

"And you drew the short straw?"

"And I was on my way to see you anyway. How'd the phone land under the bed?" she inquired, as if it weren't obvious.

He stared at her incredulously, then glanced pointedly at his bandaged hands.

If he'd expected pity or understanding, he didn't get either. She shrugged and hung up the receiver. "I suppose some people would consider that an excuse."

Frank glared at her just as the phone started to ring again. He stared at it, cursing it for the helplessness it stirred in him again. He took all of his frustration out on the therapist. "Get out!"

As skinny as she was, he was surprised his bellow alone hadn't blown her from the room. She didn't budge, every puny inch of her radiating mule-headed stubbornness. A tiny little bit of respect found its way into his perception of Ms. Jenny Michaels.

"I thought you wanted someone to answer the phone," she said, all sweet innocence over a core of what was clearly solid steel.

"I'll manage."

"How?" she said, voicing his own disgruntled thought.

"What the hell difference does it make to you?"

"I'll consider it the first step in your therapy."

She waited. He glowered, his muscles tensing with each damnable ring of the phone. Finally, thankfully, it stopped.

"It's probably just as well," she said. "It is time for your therapy. I usually like to start with something less complicated."

"Push-ups perhaps," he suggested sarcastically.

"Maybe tomorrow," she said without missing a beat. "In the meantime, why don't I just show you how to start exercising those fingers? You can repeat the exercises every hour, about ten minutes at a time."

"I'm not interested in therapy. I just want to be left alone."

Ignoring that, she ordered, "Sit," and waved him toward the bed.

"Forget it," he said, bracing himself for a fight. He'd been itching for one all morning. Everyone else had sensed that and run for their lives. Jennifer Michaels wasn't scaring so easily.

"Okay, stand," she replied, not batting an eye at his surliness. "Hold out your hand. I'll show you what I want you to do."

He backed up until he was out of reach. "What about me? What about what I want?" he thundered. "Don't you get it, lady? I'm not doing any 'exercises.'"

"You'd prefer to have your hands heal the way they are now?"

Her voice never even wavered. Frank decided in that instant that his initial impression had been right on target: Jennifer Michaels was one tough little cookie. He took another look and saw the spark of determination in her eyes. He tried again to get through that thick, do-gooder skull of hers.

"Listen, sweetheart," he said with deliberate condescension. "I know you have a job to do. I know you probably think you can accomplish miracles, but I'm not interested. The only thing I want out of life right this second is to be left alone, followed in very short order by my discharge papers."

She winced once during the tirade, but recovered quickly. After that her expression remained abso-

lutely calm. Not stoic. Not smug. *Calm.* It infuriated
him. The only people he'd ever seen that serene before had been drugged out or chanting. Around San
Francisco it was possible to see plenty of both.

"I could leave you here to stew," she said as if honestly considering the possibility. "Of course, it would
make me a lousy therapist if I let you get away with
your bullying tactics."

"I'll write you an excuse you can put in your per-
sonnel file. The patient was uncooperative and unresponsive. That ought to cover it, don't you think?"

She nodded agreeably. "It's certainly accurate
enough. Unfortunately you won't be able to hold the
pen unless you do the exercises."

"Dammit, don't you ever give up?" he said, ad-
vancing until he was towering over her. She swallowed hard, but stood her ground as he continued to
rant. "I'll type it. I ought to be able to hunt and peck,
even with my fingers like this." He waved them under
her nose for emphasis.

She leveled her green eyes at him and tried to stare
him down. When he didn't back off she shrugged.
"Suit yourself."

She headed for the door and suddenly, perversely,
Frank felt uncertain. At least she was company. And
as long as they were hurling insults, he wouldn't be
alone with his own lousy thoughts. "You're leaving?"

"That is what you said you wanted. I have patients
who are interested in getting better. I don't have time

to waste on one who's feeling sorry for himself. Think about it and we'll talk again.''

She pinned him with an unflinching green-eyed gaze until he couldn't stand it anymore. He turned away. A sigh shuddered through him as he heard the door shut softly behind her.

Well, Chambers, you definitely made a horse's ass out of yourself that time, he told himself. Not that Jennifer Michaels couldn't take it. There had been that unmistakable glint of steely determination in her eyes and an absolute lack of sympathy in her voice. At almost any other moment in his life that combination might have impressed him. He admired spunk and dedication. He was not in the habit of dishing out garbage the way he had just now, but on the occasions when his temper got the best of him, he appreciated knowing that the target had the audacity to throw it right back in his face. Jennifer Michaels had audacity to spare.

In her case, the unexpectedness of that tart, unyielding response had caught him off guard. He doubted she'd learned that particular bedside technique in therapist school. But he had to admit it was mildly effective. He felt guilty for a full five minutes before reminding himself that, like it or not, he was the patient here. Nobody was exactly coddling him.

Not that he wanted them to, he amended quickly. The papers might be calling him a hero for rescuing his co-worker, and his family might think he was behaving like a pain in the butt, but either label irked. He didn't feel particularly heroic. Nor was he ready to don

a hair shirt just because his attitude sucked. He figured he had a right. With his hands burned and his
livelihood in jeopardy, it was little wonder that his
stomach was knotted in fear. If he wanted to sulk,
then, by God, he was going to sulk, and no pint-size
therapist with freckles, saucer eyes and bright red curls
was going to cheer him up or lay a guilt trip on him.

But to his amazement, the memory of her sunny
disposition and sweet smile began to taunt him. It
couldn't be easy dealing with angry patients, some of
them injured a whole lot worse than he was. How did
she do it day after day? How much of the abuse did
she take before lashing back? How much would she
withstand before truly giving up? Somewhere deep
inside he knew that she hadn't given up on him after
this one brief skirmish. She'd only staged a tactical
retreat, leaving him with a whole lot to think about.

Frank spent the rest of the day intermittently pacing, staring at the door, waiting. Every time it opened,
his muscles tensed and his breathing seemed to go still.
Each time, when it was just a nurse or a doctor, disappointment warred with relief.

Finally, exhausted and aware that, like it or not, he
wasn't going anywhere today, he crawled back into
bed. He was stretched out on his back, counting the
tiny pinpoint holes in the water-stained ceiling tiles,
when the door opened yet again. This time he didn't
even bother turning his head.

"Hey, big brother," Tim said from the foot of the
bed. "How come you're not out chasing nurses up and

down the corridors? There are some fine-looking women around here.''

"I hadn't noticed.''

His youngest brother stepped closer, a worried expression on his face. He placed a hand against Frank's forehead. "Nope. You're not dead. Must be the smoke. It's addled you senses.''

"My senses are just fine.'' He paused. "Except maybe for touch.''

Tim chuckled. "That's better. A little humor is good for healing. I'll go tell Ma it's safe to come in now.''

"She's here?''

"They all are. They're just waiting for me to wave the white flag.''

Frank groaned. "All of them?''

"Everyone. You're the one who taught us to travel in packs in times of crisis. We're here to cheer you up. Feed you your dinner. Help with a shower. Of course, if it were me, I'd invite one of those gorgeous nurses to give me a sponge bath.''

Frank's lips twitched with a rueful smile. "I'm sure you would.''

"I know you're much too saintly to think in such terms. I'm a mere mortal, however, and I don't believe in wasting opportunities that come my way. If life hands you lemons, make—''

"I know. Make lemonade. If you ask me, too damned many opportunities have come your way,'' Frank grumbled, treading on familiar, comfortable turf. "You're like a bee in a field of wildflowers. It's a wonder you don't collapse from overexertion."

"Do you realize how many women get on a bus every single day?" his brother countered. "You want me to make an informed choice, don't you?"

"I knew I should have insisted that you work your way through law school by cutting lawns for little old ladies instead of driving a MUNI bus."

Tim stared at him thoughtfully. "I wonder if I could get them to bandage your mouth shut for a couple of weeks."

Frank sighed. "You and most of the staff around here."

"Yeah, that's what your therapist said."

Immediately interested, he searched Tim's face for some indication of his reaction to the conversation. "You talked to Jennifer Michaels?" he prodded.

"Listened is more like it. That woman can talk a mile a minute. She had plenty to say, too. I'd say you got under her skin, Brother. What did you do? Try to steal a kiss? Ma's out there trying to calm her down and convince her that at heart you're a good-natured beast worthy of saving."

"She's just frustrated because I won't do her damned exercises."

"I wouldn't mind doing a little exercising with her. She's a fox."

The observation, coming from an admitted connoisseur of the fair sex, irritated the daylights out of Frank for some reason. "Stay away from her, Timmy."

A slow, crooked grin spread across his brother's face. "I knew it. You're not dead after all. Just choosy. Actually, I think you've made an excellent choice."

"I didn't make any damned choice."

Tim went on as if he'd never uttered the denial. "Redheads are passionate. Did you know that? Fiery tempers and all that."

Frank thought about the therapist's absolute calm. "I think our Ms. Michaels may be the exception that proves the rule. She's unflappable."

"Are we talking about the same woman? Not five minutes ago she told Ma if you didn't get your butt out of this bed and down to therapy in the morning, she was going to haul you down there herself. I think she has plans for you."

The first faint stirrings of excitement sent Frank's blood rushing. "I'd like to see her try to drag me out of here," he said, a hint of menace in his tone. The truth of the matter, he suddenly realized, was that he really would like to see her do just that. If nothing else, going another round with Ms. Miracle Worker would relieve the boredom. Maybe if he tried her patience long enough, he'd witness a sampling of that fiery temper Tim claimed to have seen.

Before he could spend too much time analyzing just why that prospect appealed to him, the rest of the family crowded into the room and filled it with cheerful, good-natured teasing and boisterous arguments. Once he'd finished the tedious task of eating tasteless chicken and cold mashed potatoes with the help of his nagging sister, Frank leaned back against the pillow and let the welcome, familiar sounds lull him to sleep.

Tonight, instead of the horrible, frightening roar of a raging fire, he dreamed of a fiery redhead turning passionate in his embrace.

Jennifer Michaels could feel the tension spreading across the back of her neck and shoulders as Frank Chambers's chart came up for review at interdisciplinary rounds. The doctors and nurses on the burn unit had their say. Then it was her turn. It was a short report. In a perfectly bland voice she recited his status and his refusal to accept therapy. At least she thought she was keeping her tone neutral. Apparently she was more transparent than she'd realized.

"You sound as if that's something new," Carolanne said when rounds had ended and the others had left the therapy room. "Almost every patient balks at first, either because of the pain, because they're depressed or because they refuse to accept the seriousness of the injuries and the importance of the therapy."

Jenny sighed. She'd delivered the same lecture herself dozens of times. "I know. My brain tells me it's not my responsibility if the patient won't begin treatment, but inside it never feels right. It feels like failure."

"Must be that Catholic boarding school upbringing again. You haven't developed a full-fledged case of guilt in months now. You were overdue."

"Maybe."

The other therapist watched her closely. "Or maybe something specific about Frank Chambers gets to you."

Jenny thought of the anger in his voice, the strength in his shoulders, the coiled intensity she had sensed just beneath the surface. Then she thought of his eyes and the wounded, bemused look in them that he fought so hard to hide. He was getting to her all right. Like no patient—or no man—had in a very long time.

"I'm right, aren't I?" Carolanne persisted. "Want me to see him tomorrow? I can take over the case."

Jenny hesitated. That would be the smart thing to do, run while she had the chance. Then she thought of the lost, sorrowful expression in those compelling blue eyes.

Because she understood that sadness and fear far better than he or even Carolanne could imagine, she slowly shook her head. "No," she said finally. "Thanks, but I'll see him."

How could she possibly abandon a man who so clearly needed her—even if he couldn't admit it yet?

Two

"When am I getting out?" Frank demanded as his doctor bent over his bandages first thing in the morning. Nathan Wilding was one of the top burn specialists in the nation. In his fifties, he was compulsively dedicated, returning to the hospital at a moment's notice at the slightest sign of change in any of his patients. Occasionally gruff, and always demanding, he insisted on excellence from his staff. Because he accepted no less from himself, his staff respected him, and his patients elevated him to godlike stature. He'd been featured in almost as many San Francisco newspaper stories as 49ers quarterback Joe Montana and treated with much the same reverence. Frank considered himself lucky to be the patient of a true expert, but that didn't mean he wanted to hang around this place any longer than necessary.

"When I say so," Wilding mumbled distractedly as he carefully snipped away another layer of gauze. When the nasty wounds were fully exposed, he nodded approvingly. Personally Frank thought they looked like hell. He stared with a sort of repulsed fascination.

"Am I going to be able to work again?" he asked, furious because his voice sounded choked with fear.

"Too soon to say," Wilding replied. "Have you been doing your therapy?"

Frank evaded the doctor's penetrating gaze. He sensed the doctor already knew the answer. "Not exactly."

"I see," he said slowly, allowing the silence to go on and on until Frank met his eyes. Then he added, "I thought you wanted to get full use of your hands back."

"I do."

"Then stop giving Ms. Michaels so much grief and get to work. She's one of the best. She can help you, but only if you'll work with her."

"And if I don't?"

"Then I can't promise you'll have any significant recovery of dexterity." He pulled up a chair and sat down. "Let me spell it out for you, Mr. Chambers. Your injuries are severe, but not irreversible. Maybe even without therapy, given time, you'd be able to hold a glass again or grasp a fork, if the handle is wide enough."

He waited for that to sink in. Certain that he had Frank's full attention, he went on, "It is my understanding, however, that you are a craftsman. In fact, my wife bought one of your cabinets for our den. The workmanship is extraordinary in this day of fake wood and assembly-line furniture production. The detail is exquisite. If you ever hope to do that sort of delicate carving again, there's not a minute to waste. You'll do Ms. Michaels's exercises and follow her instructions without argument. She's a damned fine therapist. Cares about her patients. She doesn't deserve any more of your abuse."

Frank could feel an embarrassed flush creep up his neck. "She complained that I behaved like a jerk, right?"

"She didn't tell me a thing."

"Then she wrote it in the chart."

"The chart mentioned that you were uncooperative and unresponsive." Amusement suddenly danced in the doctor's eyes, chasing away the stern demeanor. "It also mentioned that you told her to write that."

As the doctor rewrapped each finger in solution-soaked gauze, he said, "Listen, I know you're frustrated and angry. It's understandable. I'd hate like hell being in your position. A doctor's not much use without his hands, either. But the fact of the matter is that you're the only thing standing in the way of your own recovery. If you think it's bad now, just wait a couple more days until the pain starts full force. You're going to hate the bunch of us, when that happens.

There's not one of us you won't think is trying to torture you. You're going to be downright nasty. You'd better hope you've made a few friends around here by then. We can walk you through it. We can remind you that the pain will pass. And Ms. Michaels can see to it that you don't let the pain make you give up and decide to find a new career that doesn't demand so much of your hands."

"In other words, it's time to stop feeling sorry for myself and get to work."

"That's about it."

The last time Frank had had a straight, no-nonsense lecture like that he'd been a teenager similarly hellbent on self-destruction. Angry over his father's death, terrified of the sudden, overwhelming responsibilities, he'd gone a little wild. He'd been creeping into the house after three in the morning, staggering drunk, when his mother had stepped out of the shadows and smacked him square on the jaw. For a little woman, she had packed a hell of a wallop.

Having convinced him just who was in charge, she had marched him into the kitchen and poured enough coffee to float a cruise ship. While he'd longed for the oblivion of sleep, she'd told him in no uncertain terms that it was time to shape up and act like a man. He'd sat at that table, miserable, unable to meet her eyes, filled with regret for the additional pain he'd inflicted on her.

And then she had hugged him and reminded him that the only things that counted in life were family and love and support in times of trouble. She'd taught him by example just what that meant. She was the most giving soul he'd ever met. Some instinct told him that deep down Jennifer Michaels might be just like her.

If he'd learned the meaning of love and responsibility from his mother, Frank had learned the meaning of strength and character from his father. Until the day he'd died of cancer, his body racked with pain, the old man had been a fighter. Reflecting on his own behavior of the past couple of days, Frank felt a faint stirring of shame. He resolved to change his tune, to cooperate with that pesky little therapist when she finally showed up again.

"She'll have no more problems with me," Frank assured the doctor. "I'll be a model patient."

Unfortunately that spirit of cooperation died the minute she walked into the room pushing a wheelchair, her expression grimly determined. He didn't even have time to reflect on how pretty she looked in the bright emerald green dress that matched her eyes. He was too busy girding himself for another totally unexpected battle.

"What's that for?" He waved his hand at the offensive contraption.

"Time for therapy," she announced cheerfully, edging the chair to the side of the bed. "Hop in, Mr. Chambers. We're going for a ride."

"Are you nuts? I'm not riding in that with some puny little wisp of a thing pushing me through the halls. My legs are just fine."

She backed the chair up a foot or so to give him room. "Let's see you move it, then. The therapy room is down the hall. I'll give you five minutes to get there." She spun on her heel and headed for the door, taking the wheelchair with her.

"Something tells me I'm not the one with the attitude problem today," he observed, still not budging from the bed, arms folded across his chest.

Jenny abandoned the wheelchair, moving so fast her rubber-soled shoes made little squeaking sounds on the linoleum. Hands on hips, she loomed over him, sparks dancing in her eyes. The soft moss shade of yesterday was suddenly all emerald fire.

"Buster, this attitude is no problem at all. If I have to bust your butt to convince you to do what you should, then that's the road I'll take. Personally I prefer to spend my time being pleasant and helpful, but I'm not above a little street fighting if that's what it takes to accomplish the job. Got it?"

Frank found himself grinning at her idea of playing down and dirty. In any sort of real street fighting, she'd be out of her league in twenty seconds. He gave her high marks for trying, though. And after what he'd put her through the previous day, he decided he owed her a round. He'd let her emerge from this particular battle unscathed.

"I'll go peacefully," he said compliantly.

She blinked in surprise, and then something that might have been relief replaced the fight in her eyes.

"Good," she said, a wonderful smile spreading across her face. That smile alone was worth the surrender. It warmed him deep inside, where he hadn't even realized he'd been feeling cold and alone.

"I had no idea how I was going to haul you into that chair if you didn't cooperate," she confided.

"Sweetheart, you should never admit a thing like that," he warned while awkwardly pulling on his robe. "Tomorrow I just might get it into my head to stand you up for this therapy date, and now I know I can get away with it."

"Who are you kidding?" she sassed right back. "You knew that anyway. You're nearly a foot taller than I am and seventy pounds heavier."

"So you admit to being all bluster."

"Not exactly." She gestured toward the door. "I have a very tall, very strong orderly waiting just outside in case my technique failed. He lifts twice your weight just for kicks."

"Which confirms that you weren't quite as sure of yourself as you wanted me to believe."

"Let's just say that I'm aware of the importance of both first impressions and contingency plans," she said as she escorted him to the door.

Outside the room she turned the wheelchair over to the orderly, who was indeed more than equal to persuading a man of Frank's size to do as he was told. "Thanks, Otis. We won't be needing this after all."

The huge black man grinned. "Never thought you would, Ms. Michaels. You're batting fifty-eight for sixty by my count. It's not even sporting fun to bet against you anymore."

"Nice record," Frank observed wryly as they walked down the hall. "I had no idea therapists kept scorecards. I'd have put up less of a fight if I'd known I was about to ruin your reputation."

"Otis is a born gambler. I'm trying to persuade him that the track is not the best place to squander his paycheck."

"So now he takes bets against you?"

"I'm hoping eventually he'll get bored enough to quit that, too. I think he's getting close." She peered up at Frank, her expression hopeful. "What do you think?"

What Frank thought, as he lost himself in those huge green eyes, was that he was facing trouble a whole lot more dangerous than the condition of his hands. His voice gentled to a near whisper. "Ms. Michaels, I think a man would be a fool to ever bet against you."

Her gaze locked with his until finally, swallowing hard, she blinked and looked away. "Jenny," she said, just as softly. "You can call me Jenny."

Frank nodded, aware that they were suddenly communicating in ways that went beyond mere words. "Jenny," he repeated for no reason other than the chance to hear her name roll off his tongue. The name was simple and uncomplicated, not at all like the woman it belonged to. He had a hunch he'd done a whole lot of miscalculating in the past couple of days. It might be fascinating to discover just how far off the mark he had been. "And I'm Frank."

"Frank."

They'd stopped outside a closed door marked Therapy and might have stood right where they were, awareness suddenly throbbing between them, if Otis hadn't strolled past, whistling, giving Jenny a conspiratorial wink. Suddenly she was all business again, opening the door, pointing to a chair. "Have a seat. I'll be right with you."

Frank stepped into a room filled with ordinary, everyday items from jars to toothbrushes, from scissors to jumbo-size crayons. He wasn't sure what he'd expected, but it certainly wasn't this dime-store collection of household paraphernalia. He hooked his foot under the rung of an ordinary straight-back chair and pulled it away from a Formica-topped table so he could sit. He eyed the assortment of equipment skeptically. He suspected his insurance was going to pay big bucks for this therapy, and for what? So he could play with a toothbrush? His spirit of cooperation took another nosedive.

"What's all this?" he asked derisively the minute Jenny joined him.

"Advanced therapy," she retorted. "If you're lucky and work hard, you'll get to it in a week or two."

He regarded her incredulously. "It's going to take two weeks before I can brush my teeth? I thought you were supposed to be good."

"I am good. You're the patient," she reminded him. "Two weeks. Could be longer. The bandages won't even be off for three weeks. Think you can handle it sooner?"

There was no mistaking the challenge. "Give me the brush," he said.

"Get it yourself."

He reached across the table and tried to pick it up. He managed it with both hands, by sliding it to the edge of the table and clamping it between his hands as it fell off. At least his quick, ball-playing reflexes hadn't suffered any.

"Now what?" Jenny said, all bright-eyed curiosity. The woman was just waiting for a failure. Frank was equally determined not to fail. He was going to set a few recovery records of his own.

He pressed harder to keep the brush from slipping and tried to maneuver it toward his mouth. "Do you have to watch every move I make?" he grumbled, sweat forming across his brow with the taxing effort.

"Yep."

Irritated by his inability to manipulate the brush and by her fascinated observation of the failure, he threw it down. "Forget it."

"Maybe we ought to work up to that," Jenny suggested mildly. There wasn't the slightest hint of gloating in her tone.

He scowled back at her, but her gaze remained unwaveringly calm. "Okay, fine," he bit out finally. "You call the shots. Where do we start?"

She sat down next to him, inching her chair so close he could smell the sweet spring scent of her perfume. "We'll start with flexing your fingers. I'll do the work this first time, okay? It's called passive motion."

Momentarily resigned, he shrugged. "Whatever you say."

With surprising gentleness, she took his hand in hers. At once Frank cursed his fate all over again. He couldn't even feel the unexpected caress. His imagination went wild though. He wondered if her skin was as soft as it looked, if the texture felt like rose petals. He was so fascinated with his fantasizing, in fact, that he barely noticed what she was doing, until she said, "Now you try it."

"Mmm?" he murmured.

She regarded him indignantly. "Frank, weren't you paying a bit of attention?"

"My mind wandered."

If she was aware of exactly where his wayward thoughts had strayed, she showed no evidence of it, not even the faintest blush of embarrassment. She picked up his other hand.

"Try to pay attention this time," she said as she slowly flexed each finger back and forth. The range of movement was minuscule. Frank couldn't believe how little she expected or how inept he was at accomplishing it. He *needed* her to move his fingers for him—and he hated that weakness.

"That's it?" he scoffed when she stopped. "That's your idea of therapy? You dragged me all the way down here for that?"

"You could have done it in your room, but we tried that routine yesterday and you didn't seem to like it. It occurred to me you might take it more seriously if I brought you down here. Just remember there's an old saying that you have to walk before you can run."

"It usually applies just to babies."

Jenny rested her hand on his forearm and regarded him intently. Compassion and understanding filled her eyes. "In this instance it might be wise if you think of your hands as being every bit as untutored as a newborn's," she told him. "The instincts are there, but the control is shaky. Right now we're just trying to assure that the joints don't stiffen up as you heal and that the skin maintains some elasticity."

Frank wasn't interested in baby steps. He wanted desperately to make strides. "All I need is to get these bandages off and I'll be just fine."

"You will be if you do the exercises religiously, ten minutes an hour. Got it?"

"I've got it."

"Want me to walk you back to your room or send for Otis?"

"Hardly. My legs aren't the problem."

"I'll be in later to check on you."

Her tone was all business and her gaze was directed at his chart as she scribbled in a notation. Frank found it thoroughly irritating that he'd apparently been summarily dismissed now that she'd gotten her way. He was just about to tell her in grumpy detail what she could do with her ridiculous therapy, when the door opened and another patient was wheeled in by the formidable Otis.

The young girl was swathed in bandages over fifty percent of her body. Only one side of her face peeked

through the gauze and only one arm remained un-
bandaged. Even so, she struggled for a smile at the
sight of Jenny. Frank felt his heart wrench at the pitiful effort.

"Hey, Pam, how's it going?" Jenny asked, her own
smile warm, her gaze unflinching.

"Pretty good. I just beat Otis at poker. He has to go
out and bring me a hamburger and fries for lunch."

Otis leaned down, his expression chagrined. "I
thought that was going to be our little secret."

Jenny chuckled. "That will teach you, big guy.
There are no secrets between therapist and patient. As
long as you're buying, you can bring me a hamburger, too."

"Women! The two of you are going to put me in the
poorhouse," the orderly grumbled, but he was grinning as he left.

Frank watched the byplay between Jenny and the
teenager for a few more minutes, irritated by their camaraderie, the easy laughter. He could feel the pull of
the warmth between them and envied it. Feeling lone-
lier than he ever had in his life, he finally slipped out
the door and went back to his room.

Late into the night, long after he probably should
have been asleep, he struggled to move his fingers just
a fraction of an inch. He wasn't sure whether he was
trying to prove something to himself . . . or to Jenny.

Three

——

Jenny had met some tough, self-defeating patients in her time, and Frank Chambers ranked right up there with the worst of them. Right now he was suffering more from wounded pride than he was from his physical injuries. A man like Frank, used to doing for others, according to his family, would hate being dependent, even temporarily. And she could tell that he was going to fight with her every step of the way, try to hide his unfamiliar weakness. She had to make him see that it took real strength to admit the need for help.

She'd once heard a burn therapist from Miami say that a patient who was a winner in life before his injury would be a winner afterward. Despite his initial surliness, she could tell that Frank Chambers was a winner. She just had to remind him of that. She had to get him past his anger and fears and on to more practical things that could speed his recovery. Sooner or later his intelligence would kick in, and he'd realize that his attitude was only hurting.

Fortunately Jenny was by nature a fighter. She'd fought her own personal demons in this very hospital, and she'd learned from the humbling experience. Sometimes that enabled her to reach patients other therapists wanted to abandon as lost causes. Knowing how easy it was to slip into despair strengthened both her compassion and her determination to keep that self-defeating slide from happening.

Yesterday, by threatening to force Frank into a wheelchair, by hinting he was worse off than he was and allowing him the victory of proving her wrong, she had won the first round. Yet it was a shaky, inconclusive victory. Today was likely to be more difficult. He was going to be expecting miracles, and if he hadn't improved overnight, he'd consider the therapy a failure and her an unwelcome intruder.

She considered sending the massive, intimidating Otis after him, but decided it would be the cowardly way out. She did take along the wheelchair though, just in case Frank needed a little extra persuasion.

Jenny breezed into the room just in time to see his breakfast tray hit the floor. She grabbed an unopened carton of milk in midair and guessed the rest. He'd gotten frustrated over his inability to cope with the milk and the utensils.

"Hey, I've heard hospital food is lousy, but that's no reason to dump it onto the floor," she said, keeping her expression neutral as he made his way from the bed to the window.

"I wouldn't know," he muttered, his rigid back to her as he stared outside. His black hair was becomingly tousled from sleep and his inability to tame it with a comb. She was touched by the sexy disarray and poked her hands in her pockets to avoid the temptation to brush an errant strand from his forehead. The shadow of dark stubble on his cheeks was equally tempting, adding to a masculine appeal she was finding it increasingly difficult to ignore.

"You could have asked for help," she said mildly.

"Dammit, woman, I am not a baby. I don't need to be fed."

"You may not be a baby, but at the moment you're acting like one. You've been burned, not incapacitated for life. There's nothing wrong with accepting a little help until you can manage on your own."

He whirled on her. "And when in hell will that be? I've been doing your damned exercises."

"Since yesterday," she reminded him.

He ignored her reasonable response, clearly determined to sulk. "Nothing's changed. I still can't even open a damned carton of milk."

She regarded him with undisguised curiosity. "Do you actually like lukewarm milk?"

"No," he admitted. "I hate the stuff."

"Then what's the big deal?"

He scowled, but she could see a faint flicker of amusement in his eyes before he carefully banked it and returned to his study of the foggy day outside. "It's the principle."

"Pretty stupid principle, if you ask me."

"Who asked you?"

"Call me generous. I like to share my opinions."

"Share them somewhere else where they're appreciated. I'm sure there are a dozen places on this corridor alone where Saint Jennifer's views would be welcomed."

The barb struck home. It wasn't the first time she'd been accused of being a Pollyanna, of nagging where she wasn't wanted. It came with the job. Even so, she had to swallow the urge to lash back. Forcing a breezy note into her voice, she said, "You probably wouldn't be nearly this cranky if you'd had your breakfast. Come on. If you don't squeal on me, I'll treat you to a couple of doughnuts and a cup of coffee in the therapy room. I guarantee there won't be anything you have to open. And the doughnuts are fresh. I stopped at the bakery on the way in."

He turned finally and regarded her warily. "Are you trying to bribe me into coming back to therapy?"

"I'm trying to improve your temper for the benefit of the entire staff on this floor. Now come along."

Blue eyes, which had been bleak with exhaustion and defeat, sparked briefly with sheer devilment. "Do I have a choice?" he inquired, his voice suddenly filled with a lazy challenge.

"You do, but just so you know, the wheelchair's right outside."

"And Otis?"

"He's within shouting distance, but I didn't think I'd need him today." Her gaze held a challenge of its own. She could practically see the emotions warring inside him as he considered his options. She pressed a little harder. "So, are you coming or not? I have jelly doughnuts. Or chocolate. There's even one that's apple-filled."

Temptation won out over stubbornness. She could see it in the suddenly resigned set of his shoulders. Apparently she'd hit on a weakness with those doughnuts.

"You are a bully," he accused, but he followed her from the room.

"Takes one to know one. What's it going to be jelly, chocolate or apple?"

"Jelly, of course. You could probably see my mouth watering the minute you mentioned them."

"I did sense I had your attention."

"Why do you do this?" he asked as they walked down the hall.

"Buy doughnuts?"

The evasion earned a look of disgust. "You know what I meant."

"They pay me to do it."

"So you've said. I'm more interested in why someone would choose a profession that requires them to put up with nasty-tempered patients like me."

"Maybe I'm a masochist."

"I don't think so. What's the truth, Jenny Michaels?"

There was a genuine curiosity in his eyes that demanded an honest response. "Sometimes," she said softly, "sometimes I can make a difference."

He nodded at once with obvious understanding. "Quite a high, huh?"

She grinned at the way he mirrored her thoughts. "Quite a high."

He glanced sideways at her. "I'd guess the lows are pretty bad, though."

Jenny sobered at once, thinking of the patients who struggled and lost against insurmountable odds. "Bad enough."

Inside the sunshine-bright therapy room, she put two jelly doughnuts on a plate and poured a cup of coffee for Frank as he nudged a chair up to the table with some deft footwork. She sat beside him and encouraged him to talk about himself. As he did, almost without him realizing, she broke off bits of the doughnuts and fed them to him. More than once her fingers skimmed his lips, sending a jolt of electricity clear through her. He seemed entirely unaware of it, thank goodness.

"So you worked odd jobs from the time you were a kid and helped your mother raise all of those handsome characters I've met," she said.

"You think they're handsome?" he asked, watching her suspiciously. "All of them?"

She nodded, playing on the surprising hint of vulnerability she detected. "One of them is a real charmer, too. What's his name? Tim?"

"He's a little young for you, isn't he?" he inquired, his gaze narrowed, his expression sour.

Jenny chuckled at his obviously suspicious response to her teasing. "Who are you looking out for? Him or me?" She decided not to mention the third alternative, Frank himself.

"You. Tim learned to take care of his own social life long ago. It's very active."

"And yours?"

He suddenly looked uncomfortable. "Not so active, at least not lately."

"Why not? You're the best-looking one in the bunch," she said. She wasn't above using flattery to get her way, but in his case it wasn't necessary. Frank Chambers had a quiet strength and serenity about him when he wasn't raging at the universe. He seemed like the kind of man a woman could depend on. And everything she'd heard about him from his adoring family confirmed that. Plus, his slightly crooked nose, the firm, stubborn line of his jaw and the astonishingly blue eyes gave his face a rugged appeal. She'd always preferred that type to the polished professionals in their designer shirts, designer watches and phony smiles. In Frank's case the internal strength and diamond-in-the-rough exterior added up to a potent and very masculine combination.

"I'm astonished no woman has snapped you up," she said with honesty, wondering as she did so why she felt so glad that he was free and unencumbered. She never got involved with her patients. Lately, in fact, she never got involved with any man. Keeping her tone light and bantering, she added, "You're obviously domesticated. You probably even do dishes."

He shook his head adamantly. "Oh, no. Not if I can help it. That's probably the single greatest advantage I can think of having so many younger brothers and a baby sister. When I was younger, my turn to do dishes only came about once a week. If I was really on my toes, I'd land a job mowing lawns whenever it was my turn, or bribe one of the others to take it. Karyn earned more doing dishes for me than she ever did baby-sitting."

Suddenly his gaze fell on the empty plate and coffee cup. His expression became perplexed. "How'd you do that?"

She grinned at him. "It's all a matter of technique."

"That kind of sleight of hand belongs on stage."

"Hey, for all you know, I ate it all myself."

"Not a chance."

"How come?"

Before she realized what he intended, he scooted his chair closer, reached over and brushed the tip of one bandaged finger across her lips. The gauze tickled, but there was nothing humorous about the emotional impact. Jenny felt the sizzle of that touch somewhere deep inside. "No jelly," he said softly. "No powdered sugar." He looked suddenly regretful. "I almost wish there were."

"Why?" she said in a voice that trembled as she lost herself to the intensity of his gaze.

"So I could see if it tastes even sweeter on you."

Jenny's pulse skittered wildly. She swallowed hard and dragged her gaze away. Countering the rush of unexpected feelings, she was suddenly all business.

"Talk about distractions," she murmured, partly to herself. The sizzling tension shattered like fragile glass as she injected an energetic note into her voice. "All this talk has kept you from your therapy. Let's get to work. Do something a little more challenging. Try squeezing this washcloth."

She handed him a cloth that had been folded into a thick rectangular wad. With infinite patience, she closed his hand around it. It would be days before he could complete the closure, days before the tips of his fingers could comfortably touch his own palm.

Frank, obviously, didn't understand the difficulty. He shot her a look of pure disgust. "Any two-year-old can do that," he said, obviously ignoring the difficulty of yesterday's even less taxing assignment.

"Then it should be a breeze for you."

She deliberately turned her back on him, sat at her desk and attacked her paperwork. When his cursing turned the air blue, she smiled, but she didn't give an inch.

"You're doing this just to break my spirit," he muttered finally.

Jenny glanced up and saw the furrows in his brow as he struggled with the simple task. "Mr. Chambers..."

"Frank, dammit!"

"Frank," she said quietly, countering irritation with determined calm. "A rodeo bronc rider couldn't break your spirit. What I'm going for here is a little spirit of cooperation."

"Right," he muttered between gritted teeth. But when the time came for him to return to his room, she had almost as much trouble getting him to leave as she'd had getting him there in the first place.

Something astonishing had happened to Frank in that therapy room, while doing those ridiculous yet nearly impossible exercises. He'd decided to fight. Not in some half-baked way, either, but with everything in him. Maybe it was because the prospect of doing anything else didn't sit well with a man used to being firmly in control of his own life. Maybe the smoke had finally cleared from his brain so he could see things straight again.

Or maybe it was just that one flash of insight he'd had, when he'd realized that he'd do almost anything to earn Jenny's approval, to win one of her warm and tender smiles. He'd searched a long time to find a woman who was part hellion and part angel. And something told him he'd finally found her.

He was back in his room, still squeezing the devil out of that washcloth, when his mother turned up. He smiled at her entrance. She was sixty-two now and her once-raven hair had turned gray, but nothing had daunted her spirit. She came in with all the bustle of the briskest nurse on the floor.

"You've eaten your lunch?" she said, fussing around him.

"Hours ago," he said, resigned to the straightening of the sheets, the rearrangement of the flowers crowded on top of the room's small dresser, the quick check of the trash can to assure that the housekeeping staff was on its toes.

"Brushed your teeth?" She straightened up the things on his nightstand. Flicking away some invisible speck of lint.

He endured the bustling activity as long as he could, then said, "Ma, settle down."

Not used to being still, she spent about ten seconds in the chair by the bed before she was up again, fiddling with the blinds until they let in the pale light of the sun as it burned off the last of the day's fog. "You still giving that therapist trouble?"

"No."

She nodded. "Good." She shot him a pointed look. "She seems like a nice girl."

"She is."

"Pretty, too."

The description was far too bland to describe Jenny, but he nodded anyway. "Yes. What's your point?"

Shrewd blue eyes danced with amusement. "If you can't figure that one out, boy, there's no hope for you."

Frank nearly groaned aloud. If his mother got it into her head to play matchmaker, neither he nor Jenny would have another moment's peace. "Stay out of it, Ma."

The remark was met with startled innocence. "Out of what? I was just making an observation."

"Your *observation* is duly noted."

"Is she married?"

"Ma!"

"Okay, okay, you do what you want. You're not like your brothers. They're always looking. Saturday night doesn't pass, they're not out with this one or that one. There are times I think I did you a terrible disservice by giving you so much responsibility. Maybe you think you've already finished raising your family. I just thought maybe you needed reminding that Karyn and your brothers aren't the same as having a wife and kids of your own."

"Believe me, I'm aware of that."

"Are you really? You didn't exactly rush into marrying Megan. Kept her dangling long enough."

At the mention of his ex-fiancée's name, Frank felt a familiar tightness in his chest. "I don't want to talk about Megan."

"That's the trouble. You never did. You kept it all bottled up inside. Five years you dated that woman and then, poof, it was over. You never did say what happened, not even which one of you broke it off."

"And I don't intend to say so now. Megan is history."

"Then let's get back to the present. When are you seeing this Jenny again?"

"Ma!" The muttered warning gave way to a chuckle. "You're incorrigible."

She bent over and planted a kiss on his cheek. "There, then, that's much better. It's good to see you laughing again, Son. I've been worried about you. You've been entirely too glum these past few days."

"I'll survive."

"I know that. Even when you were a little boy, you were a survivor. Of all my kids, you were the one who never shed a tear. Your father used to say you'd been born with a stiff upper lip."

"Not so stiff," he countered. "Half the time, it was split from losing control of my bike on the hills and slamming into some wall or car."

They were laughing at the memories when Jenny came by. Frank saw her hesitate in the doorway. "You can come in."

"I'm so used to hearing shouts from this room, I wasn't quite sure what to make of this new cheerful sound. Thought for sure I had to be in the wrong place."

Frank caught the beaming smile of welcome on his mother's face, the speculative gleam in her eyes.

"Come on in, child. We were just talking over old times," his mother said.

"I could come back later," Jenny offered.

"No, indeed," his mother said. "You sit right over here." She shoved the room's only chair even closer to the side of the bed. "I think maybe I'll go get myself a cup of coffee."

Jenny backed away a step. "Really, it's not necessary. Maybe if you stick around, he won't grumble quite so much about the therapy."

"Don't you believe it. He enjoys shocking me with his language. He knows he's gotten too big for me to wash his mouth out with soap."

"Ma, you never once washed my mouth out with soap," Frank protested, enjoying the expression of amusement on Jenny's face.

"Only because you didn't use any of those foul words until you knew you outweighed me."

Frank turned to Jenny. "Don't believe her 'poor, pitiful me' act. She wouldn't hesitate to take on any one of us no matter our size or our age."

"That's the truth," Kevin said coming through the door just then. "She may be tiny, but she has us all cowed."

"Says you," Tim scoffed, entering right on his brother's heels. "I'm not scared of Ma."

Mrs. Chambers drew herself up to her full height, which was about as intimidating as a sparrow's. "Well, you ought to be, young man," she said sternly. "Where were you last night?"

Tim immediately blushed furiously. Avoiding Jenny's laughter-filled eyes, he said meekly, "I had a date."

"What kind of date lasts until three a.m.?"

"Whoa," Frank said, enjoying seeing Tim squirm. "Now you're going to catch it, baby brother. You know what Ma's like when she doesn't get her beauty rest."

Tim gave a dramatic shrug. He slid his arm around Jenny's waist. "Since I'm already in hot water, what are you doing tonight?"

"She's going home," Frank said, suddenly no longer amused.

Jenny's gaze shot to him, and her lips formed a mutinous frown. "Oh, really? Who made you the keeper of my social calendar?"

Frank's eyes narrowed. His voice dropped. "Do you want to go out with him?"

"Oh, for heaven's sake," she said with a shake of her head that set her curls bounding indignantly. "Whether I do or I don't is not something I intend to discuss in front of a roomful of people."

"We could go outside," Tim said at once, his eyes bright with mischief.

"You do and I'll be right behind you," Frank countered.

His gaze locked with his brother's. In that instant of masculine challenge, a clear message was sent and received. Tim draped an arm around his mother's shoulders. "Come on, Ma, I guess it's you and me, after all. Kevin, you, too."

"But we just got here," Kevin grumbled.

"Now," Tim said with the kind of firm diplomacy that would have made him the perfect State Department emissary. Of course, the family liked to tease him that by the time he finished law school, he'd probably be too old to board a plane, anyway.

Blessed silence descended the minute they were gone. Jenny began inching backward toward the door.

"Sometimes, they're a little overwhelming," Frank said. "But they mean well."

"I can see that."

"Did you come by for a reason?"

"I just wanted to check and see how things were going with your therapy before I took off for the night. They should be in soon with your dinner tray."

"Do you follow all your patients this closely?"

There was no mistaking the hint of pink that tinted her cheeks. "As a matter of fact, I do."

"Then why does it bother you that I asked the question?"

"Who says it bothers me? Look, if you're okay, I'll be on my way."

"I'd be a lot better if you'd stick around."

"And do what?"

"Talk to me."

"Your family could do that. Why'd you chase them out?"

"I didn't chase. They left. Besides, they talk to me all the time. I've heard all their stories. I'd like to hear yours."

Jenny sighed, but she stopped inching toward the door. "My stories aren't all that fascinating."

"They would be to me."

She stared at him, her brow knit by a puzzled frown. "Why?"

"Does there have to be a specific reason?"

"There usually is," she said with a distinct trace of cynicism.

"I'm not exactly likely to put any moves on you," he said, holding up his bandaged hands.

The remark earned him a genuine chuckle. "True."

"Then there's nothing to be afraid of, is there?" Frank wasn't sure why he was pushing or why she was so afraid. He only knew it was important to his soul in some elemental way to keep her from leaving. When she finally sat, even though she kept the chair a careful distance away, he breathed a sigh of relief.

"So, Jenny Michaels, exactly what makes you tick?"

Four

Frank scowled at the ringing phone. How the devil was any man with five interfering brothers and one doting sister supposed to get to know a woman? he wondered as the phone rang for the third time in the hour since he'd encouraged Jenny to tell him all about herself. It was not the first time in his adult life that he'd been faced with the dilemma. Which was probably why it had taken him five years to figure out that Megan was the wrong woman for him and another two months to let her down gently. She'd fit in so well with the entire family, he hadn't noticed until too late that she didn't suit him. He had no intention of making the same mistake again.

"Karyn," he told his sister after listening to five minutes of household-repair questions, "I love you dearly, but why are you asking me how to fix the sink, when you have a perfectly good husband? Is Brad out?"

He glanced over and caught Jenny's amused expression. Rather than seeming frustrated by the nonstop interruptions, she appeared relieved. In fact, she seemed to enjoy them. She tucked the receiver between his chin and his shoulder each time and eavesdropped blatantly.

"No, but my husband races sports cars and sells ritzy sedans," Karyn retorted. "What makes you think he knows anything about sinks? Talk about sexist remarks."

"Any man who can tear a carburetor apart and put it back together again in five minutes flat ought to be able to open a trap under the sink and clean out whatever's stopping up the drain. For that matter, you ought to be able to do it yourself."

Karyn sighed heavily. "With six brothers in the house, who needed to learn?"

"Now who's being sexist?"

"Never mind. I'll call the plumber."

"Are you sure the sink's actually clogged?" he inquired suspiciously.

"Well, of course it is. Why else would I call?"

"Maybe you just don't want me to feel useless while I'm lying here in my hospital bed."

"Frank Chambers, I am standing here in an inch of water and you're accusing me of lying?"

"It wouldn't be the first time, Toots. I love you for trying, though. See you tomorrow."

He heard her indignant huff as he signaled to Jenny to put the phone back in its cradle. "I swear to you I didn't ask you to stay just so you could answer the phone."

"It's okay. I love seeing you with your family. How many are there again? When they're all here, it seems like dozens."

"Five brothers. One sister. One brother-in-law. All trouble."

She studied him thoughtfully, her green eyes intent. "Something tells me you don't really mind," she said after a thorough examination that nearly left him breathless, despite its innocence. Never before had he been with a woman who had the uncanny ability to see inside his soul.

"Am I that transparent?"

Apparently she detected the nervousness in his voice, because she laughed and reassured him. "No, it's actually something you said the other day. You understood what I meant about making a difference, about being needed."

"You get the same fix from your patients."

"Absolutely."

"No brothers or sisters?"

"Nope. I'm an only child. My parents live back East. I don't see them that often."

Frank couldn't imagine what it was like for her being separated from the only family she had. For all his grumbling, he rarely went more than a day without dropping in to see his mother or one of the other members of the tight-knit Chambers clan. They all checked in daily by phone, just to touch base, exchange news or seek advice. To his occasional regret, the latter was growing increasingly rare.

"Don't you miss your parents?" he asked Jenny.

"Yes, but we were never as close as your family is. We love each other, and they're great people, but they raised me to be independent. When the time came, they nudged me out of the nest just like a mother bird does. None of us has ever looked back. Holidays generally give us enough time to catch up."

The phone rang again. Frank glowered at it. "Tell 'em I've gone to Tahiti," he suggested.

"You wish," Jenny countered, answering it and then putting the receiver next to his ear.

"Well, well," Jared said. "Look who's answering your phone at seven o'clock at night. Does she get overtime for that?"

Frank scanned Jenny's face to see if she'd overheard the teasing comment with its sly innuendo. She seemed awfully intent suddenly on settling just so in the chair by his bed. She smoothed her dress over her knees, crossed her legs, smoothed her dress again.

"She's not a nurse, and cut the jokes," he muttered to his irreverent brother. "Did you call for a reason?"

"I take it I'm interrupting something," he said with delight. "Did you share a cozy dinner of Jell-O? Maybe some fruit cocktail?"

"You always were the perceptive one. Why aren't you hanging up?"

"You've got me mixed up with Tim." Jared went blithely on, refusing to take the hint. "Want to talk about what color you'd like me to paint your house? I thought I'd take a couple of days off work and work on it. We've been talking about it for a while now. I was thinking something cheery, maybe bright yellow."

The thought horrified Frank sufficiently to draw his attention away from the fascinating way Jenny's dress clung to her curves. He knew that Jared was perfectly capable of slapping on the most outrageous shade of paint he could find. The walls in his own apartment were the color of tangerines. The year before his bedroom had been neon green until his girlfriend rebelled. Frank did not want Jared near his house with a paintbrush unless he was on hand to watch every move and to inspect the bucket of paint.

"You paint my house yellow and it will seriously impair any plans you might have for a future family life," he warned as emphatically and discreetly as he could. Jenny's eyes danced with merriment.

"Okay, no yellow," Jared said agreeably. "How about mauve? Maybe with green trim."

Frank groaned. "And have the place look like a damned bouquet of violets? You've got to be kidding. Do we have to discuss this now?"

"Absolutely not. We don't have to discuss it at all. I can choose."

"Good God, no! How about white? Simple, straightforward, normal."

"Boring," Jared retorted succinctly.

Frank glanced at Jenny. "What's your favorite color?"

"Blue," she said without hesitation. "Why?"

"The lady says blue. Bring the paint chips by tomorrow and we'll decide on the shade. Now go away."

Jared chuckled. "Your seduction technique has taken a fascinating turn, big brother. I wonder how Ma'd feel if she knew you were painting your house to impress a woman. She'd probably start ordering wedding invitations. Should I pass on this startling development?"

"Go to hell."

"Night, pal."

This time Jenny was slow to hang up the phone. Her expression was a mix of curiosity and astonishment. "You're going to paint your house blue on a whim?"

"Actually Jared's going to paint it."

"You know what I mean."

"It needs to be painted. Blue's as good a color as any," he said, determinedly making light of his decision to pick a color that might please her. He wasn't entirely sure himself why he'd done it. "With white trim. What do you think?"

"I think you're nuts."

"Don't say that to Dr. Wilding. He'll find some shrink and send him in for a consult."

The night nurse poked her head in just then. "You want anything to help you sleep tonight?"

Frank shook his head. "Nope," he said, glancing straight at Jenny. "Something tells me I'm going to have very pleasant dreams."

He held her gaze until he could see the slow rise of heat that turned her cheeks a becoming shade of pink. For some reason he enjoyed the thought that he could fluster the usually unflappable therapist.

"Maybe I'd better get out of here and let you rest," she said, clearly nervous at the intimate turn the conversation had taken.

Instinctively he reached for her hand, then realized he couldn't grasp it in his gauze-covered mitts. He drew his hand back, but held her in place with the sheer force of his will. "Don't go, please. It gets too damned lonely around here."

She shook her head. "I can't stay."

"You have plans?"

"No, not exactly."

She looked so miserable, he finally relented. "I'm sorry. It was selfish of me to ask. You probably can't wait to shake this place at the end of the day."

"It's not that. It's just that this..."

"This?"

"Being here with you, it's not such a good idea. I should never have stayed."

"Will it make the other patients jealous?" he teased.

Suddenly she looked angry. "Don't act as if you don't know what I mean," she said, marching toward the door. He could read the conflicting emotions warring on her face as she cast one last helpless look at him and left.

"Sweet dreams," he murmured.

Frank's dreams, however, were anything but sweet. He awoke in the early hours of the morning to the slow return of sensation in his hands. At first there were just tiny pinpricks of feeling. In no time, though, his hands felt as if someone had stripped off the skin and dipped them in acid. The excruciating pain blocked out everything else.

In agony he fumbled for the call bell and tried to press it. The effort cost him all his reserves of energy, and he wasn't even sure he'd succeeded in rousing anyone at the nurses' station. As he waited, he sank back against the pillow and tried to fix a picture of Jenny in his mind. Her image brought him some small measure of comfort as he fought to hypnotize himself against the pain.

He couldn't say that Dr. Wilding hadn't warned him. He'd always held the mistaken notion that healing meant an end to pain. In the case of burns, however, he was just discovering that the healing of the nerve endings brought with it a nearly unbearable torture.

The door opened and one of the night nurses peeked in. "You okay?"

"I've had better nights," he said, his teeth gritted together.

Her relaxed, middle-of-the-night composure was instantly transformed into alert briskness. "Pain," she said at once. "I'll be right back. There's an order in your chart."

The five minutes it took her to get the medication and bring it back were the longest of Frank's life. Even the shot, with its promise of relief, brought no immediate change. Nor did the nurse's soothing words. He tried to remember all those spills from his bike that he'd survived so stoically, but none had affected him like this. Nothing had ever hurt like this.

The door whispered open, but with his eyes clamped shut he couldn't tell if someone had come in, or if the nurse had simply left. Suddenly the scent of spring flowers seemed to fill the room. Jenny!

He opened his eyes. "What are you doing here at this hour? It must be three or four in the morning." He winced as his hands throbbed.

Still wearing the same bright silk dress she'd had on earlier, she came closer. With cool, soothing fingers, she caressed his brow. "It won't be long now before the shot kicks in. Think about something quiet and peaceful."

Her voice was low, hypnotic, but he fought the effect. He had to tell her…something. His aching hands kept interfering. He fought the pain as he tried to capture the elusive thought.

"You knew, didn't you?" he said finally.

"Knew what?"

"That the pain might start tonight. That's why you stayed."

She didn't bother denying it, just pressed a finger to his lips. "Quiet. Close your eyes."

Frank didn't want to close his eyes. He wanted to keep staring at the woman who cared so much that she'd spent the night at the hospital on the off chance she might be needed. Despite his efforts, though, the medication began to take hold and he found himself fading out. He fought for one last glimpse of Jenny, who'd drawn the chair close beside him and was gently rubbing his arm. Maybe his own weary eyes were playing tricks on him, but it seemed for just an instant that he could see tears shimmering on her lashes.

He reached out to her, found her hand and touched her gently. "Thank you."

At last he was able to relax into the pain, rather than fight it. Finally, thankfully, the pain dimmed and he fell asleep. This time his dreams were sweet indeed.

Every therapy session over the next couple of days was torture for the both of them. It made the fire and those first days of exercise seem like child's play. Though Frank was in agony, he was stubborn. His therapy sessions were scheduled right after the dressing changes when the medication was in full force, and he was determined not to miss one. Jenny was equally unrelenting. She pushed, and pushed some more. He had to admire her spunk, even as he sometimes cursed her dedication and his own weakness.

He couldn't have pinpointed the precise moment when his feelings for Jenny began to change into something more than respect, when her magnificent, gentle spirit invaded his soul and made him whole again. Maybe it was when she was giving him hell.

Maybe it was when she touched his bandaged hands with a gentleness that took his breath away. Maybe it was when he caught the glitter of tears in her eyes, when his pain was just this side of unbearable and neither of them backed away from it. Maybe it was simply when she sat by his bed and talked him through the endless nights. He didn't know quite what to make of the new feelings, but they were there and growing hour by hour.

"Go home," he said after the third night, when she'd stayed with him yet again. "You look lousy."

"Flattery will win me over every time." Her tone was light, but there was no mistaking the exhaustion in her eyes, the pallor of her skin. Even her bouncy red curls seemed limp.

"I'm not interested in flattering you. I'm interested in seeing you get some sleep. You can't stay awake with me and then turn around and work all day."

"I'm okay. I get home for an hour or so in the morning to take a shower and change. Then I sneak in naps in the staff lounge."

"Well, that certainly eases my mind," he said dryly. "Jenny, go home. If you don't, I'll skip therapy, my hands will heal like this and you'll be to blame."

"Oh, no, you don't," she countered. "I'm not falling into that trap. I didn't burn you and I'm not responsible for your recovery. My only obligation is to show you the way to get your strength and dexterity back. What you do with that information is up to you."

"Tell me, does this treatment you're obliged to provide include being mean and nasty?"

"When it's called for."

He grinned. "You think you're pretty tough, don't you?"

"Tough enough."

"Oh, Jenny, I hope you never figure out what a marshmallow you really are."

"A marshmallow?" she said indignantly. "You're not in here wallowing in self-pity anymore, are you?"

"No."

"And who badgered you out of it?"

"You did," he said dutifully. "But, lady, you don't know the meaning of badgering until you've seen what I'm capable of. Go home."

Her chin rose a stubborn notch. "And if I don't?"

"I have the name and number of the director of physical therapy right here." He patted the pocket of the pajamas he'd had Jared bring him when he could stand the flapping, indecent hospital gown no longer.

Those impudent, saucer eyes of hers widened. "You wouldn't dare," she said.

He folded his arms across his chest and grinned. "Just try me."

"That's blackmail."

"I prefer to think of it as tough love."

At the mention of love, Jenny went absolutely still. Her previous serene eyes were filled with a riot of emotions. "You're breaking that vow."

"What vow? I don't remember any vow. You must be hallucinating. Due to lack of sleep, no doubt."

"In this very room. Two nights ago. You were muttering in your sleep."

"Ahh," he said knowingly. "So, now I'm the one who was asleep. You can't hold me accountable for what I said then."

She glared at him. "You woke up and said . . . something."

"And what did you say to this incredible declaration of . . . something?"

"I told you that all patients feel that way."

His gaze narrowed. "*All patients?* I am not just any old patient, Jennifer Michaels."

She sighed heavily. "I didn't mean it that way. Why are you doing this? You swore you'd drop this crazy idea that you . . ." She hesitated, stumbling over the obvious word. "That you like me."

Frank did not recall a single word of the conversation she was describing, but that didn't mean it hadn't happened. The words seemed to reflect all too clearly the thoughts that had been on his mind a lot the past few days.

"*Like?*" he repeated. "Now there's a word without much oomph. No, Jenny Michaels, I can't say I *like* you." His low, suggestive tone left no doubt as to an alternative word choice.

"I'm leaving," she said at once.

His grin broadened. "Now I know the trick," he said smugly. "Mention love and you run like a scared rabbit."

"Nobody in this room mentioned love," she retorted. "And no one will, if they have a bit of sense."

"Yes, ma'am," Frank said as she stalked from the room.

But it was pretty damned hard not to fall in love with a woman with that much sheer audacity. He'd just have to keep his feelings to himself until it suited him—and her—to make them perfectly clear. While he was still in the hospital was not the time, but soon, though. *Very soon.*

Five

"Hey, Otis! You got a break coming up?" Frank called out as the orderly passed his room pushing Pam to her therapy session. Otis paused, and the teenager gave Frank one of those wobbly smiles that came close to breaking his heart. He winked at her.

"In thirty minutes, why?" Otis said.

"I've got a deck of cards. Care to try a little five-card stud?"

Otis's eyes lighted up. "Stakes?"

"Matchsticks. Aspirin. Nickle-dime. Whatever."

A little of the gambling enthusiasm waned. "Better than nothing, I guess. Where'd you get the cards?"

"My sister. I told her I wanted to play gin rummy."

"Ah, a devious man after my own heart."

Frank shook his head. "No, a man who is bored to tears. Do you know how outrageous daytime television is? I'm not sure I could watch one more talk show deal with men who like to wear ladies' panties or women who've been tortured by drug-addicted kids. It's giving me a very peculiar and very depressing view of society. I will even stoop to luring you into a poker game to escape watching another one of those illuminating discussions. God will no doubt punish me for my sins and for my shortsightedness about society's ills."

"I don't know about God, man, but Jenny's gonna have your hide." Otis chuckled. "Mine, too. I'll be back in a flash."

"Wait a sec," Pam said, a glint of mischief in her eyes. "I want to play, too."

Frank and Otis exchanged a look. "I don't know," Frank said. "Leading Otis down the road to perdition is one thing, but you're just a kid."

"A kid on her way to therapy," she reminded them pointedly, her dark brown eyes very serious.

"Meaning what?" Frank countered, trying to contain a grin at her blatant blackmail tactics.

"Meaning she'll blab her head off if we don't say yes," Otis grumbled. "She and Jenny are thick as thieves." He peered down at her. "You know, Pam-e-la, I just might decide to park you in a linen closet and forget where I've left you."

"You wouldn't dare," she said knowingly. "If Doc Wilding found out, he'd make you pay him back that ten you borrowed to bet on the Giants' opening-day game. A game they lost, in case you've forgotten."

"For a skinny kid who's confined to a bed, you sure know a lot," Otis grumbled.

"Enough," she said proudly. "This place has more gossip than *General Hospital.*"

"Okay, say we let you play," Frank said, studying the teenager. "You any good?"

"I can hold my own," she said with what was probably sheer bravado. Even wrapped in gauze bandages, she managed a jaunty demeanor.

"You know a straight from a full house?"

"I know the full house wins. Four of a kind and straight flush beat that."

Frank grinned and relented, which he'd known he was going to do from the moment she'd asked. Nobody could refuse a kid like Pam, who was trying so hard to be brave and upbeat. "Be in my room in thirty minutes."

Pam beamed. "You bet. Otis, don't you dare forget to pick me up in the therapy room."

The orderly shook his head. "No, ma'am. Wouldn't dream of it." He looked at Frank. "Something tells me the kid here is gonna mop the floor with the two of us."

"I'm not worried," Frank said. Not about Pam, anyway. However, he was just the teensiest bit concerned about what Jenny was going to have to say if she ever found out about the card game.

There was approximately ten dollars in change piled in front of Pam when he found out exactly how Jenny would react. His own neat stacks of nickels and dimes had been dwindling almost as rapidly as Otis's. It didn't matter since Jenny sent the entire supply of change flying with one sweep of her arm. The coins rained down like sleet, tinkling on the linoleum and rolling every which way.

"You two should be ashamed of yourselves," she said, glaring from Frank to Otis and back again, her hands on her hips.

"What about her?" Otis grumbled, turning an indignant look on Pam.

"I was winning!" the teenager protested accusingly to Jenny. "Why'd you do that? I almost had enough to buy two new magazines and a box of candy from the gray ladies this afternoon."

Jenny looked defeated and miserable. She sank down on the side of the bed. "I don't believe this. You've corrupted her."

"Corrupted her?" Frank said. "I'd like to know how. The girl has the instincts of a Las Vegas house dealer. She's a shark."

Pam looked pleased. Jenny didn't.

"And that makes it right?" Jenny snapped. "Couldn't you have played just for fun?"

"This was fun," Frank countered reasonably.

"But you lost how much?"

"A couple of bucks, less than I would have spent to go to a movie, and I can't even get to a movie."

"What about you?" she said to Otis.

"About the same."

"And added to what you've lost this week, how much does that make it?"

Frank interrupted before Otis could respond. "Look, it's my fault, okay? I was bored. I suggested the game. A little cash made it more interesting. That doesn't mean we're all candidates for Gambler's Anonymous."

"Maybe not you and Pam," she said pointedly.

Otis rose slowly to his feet. He glowered down at her. With his size, it would have made Frank think twice about arguing with him. It didn't daunt Jenny in the slightest.

"Don't you try to intimidate me, Otis Johnson," she said. "I thought you wanted to buy a new car, find a nicer apartment. How do you expect to do that if you keep losing your shirt on these crazy bets. Dammit, Otis, you promised."

It seemed a lot of people were making promises to Jenny that they weren't keeping. Frank almost felt sorry for her, but he wasn't sure what all the fuss was about. Making a few bets was no big deal.

"Ain't nothing crazy about betting on a flush, king-high," Otis grumbled.

"Did you win?"

"The kid had a full house. What can I say?"

Jenny sighed. "I don't get it. Where's the fun in throwing away your money like that?"

"Stick around and I'll show you," Frank offered.

"I'm not betting one dime in a card game."

"You won't have to," he promised. He exchanged a look with Otis who apparently guessed his intentions. The orderly suddenly glanced at his watch.

"Break's over," the orderly said hurriedly. "Come on, Pam, I'll give you a push back to your room. Leave those coins on the floor. I'll pick 'em up later."

"And bring me my share," Pam warned.

"Don't worry, kid. You'll get what's coming to you," he promised.

When they'd gone, Frank waved Jenny toward a chair. "Take a seat." He nodded toward the cards. "You'll have to shuffle and deal. Just sit the cards in this contraption Otis rigged up."

She scowled at him. "This is ridiculous."

"You wanted to see why we think poker's so much fun. I'm going to show you. Deal. Five cards."

He watched the way Jenny handled the cards and suddenly the temperature in the room seemed to soar about ten steamy degrees. He imagined those strong, supple hands working their magic on him. The effect on his body was immediate and downright uncomfortable. If Jenny had any idea of what the stakes were now, she'd have run for her life. Instead she shuffled intently.

"You might consider locking the door," he said blithely.

She shot him a startled look. "Why?"

"The game I had in mind isn't meant for observers."

Her gaze narrowed suspiciously. "I thought we were playing poker."

"We are. Strip poker."

The cards hit the table with a smack. Her eyes flashed dangerously. "Oh no you don't, Frank Chambers. Are you out of your mind?"

"What's the matter?" he inquired innocently. "Chicken? You have to admit it would be a whole lot more fascinating than nickles and dimes."

"In your dreams."

He nodded cheerfully. "That's as good a place as any to start."

She bundled up the deck of cards and stalked to the door. "If I catch you trying to lead Otis and Pam astray again, I'll..." She seemed suddenly at a loss for words.

"What?" he taunted, grinning.

"I don't know, but you won't like it."

His smile widened. "Bet I will."

"You are impossible."

"You wouldn't want to bet on that, would you?"

Jenny groaned. "I think maybe I liked you better when you were surly and unresponsive."

"That's just because you don't trust yourself around me now."

"Oh, no," she said. "That's where you're wrong. In fact, that's one bet I'd take you up on."

"Liar," he taunted, but he said it to her back just before the door slammed behind her.

Okay, so she lied. Jenny wasn't quite sure what to make of this mellower Frank Chambers or her own response to him. Though his initial anger had impeded his progress at times, at least it was an emotion she understood. Now, suddenly, his personality had undergone a complete turnaround. He was joking with the staff, playing cards with Otis, no longer badgering the doctors for his release. He was hardly meek, but he was cooperative. She should have been grateful. Instead she was scared to death. He spent so much time in the therapy room these days, he could have taken over with the other patients. Whenever he was there, she had trouble concentrating. Her gaze kept shifting to him, and each time it did, her pulse raced.

As a patient in trouble, Frank had been someone in need of caring, in need of her help. Now she could no longer ignore the warm-as-honey, deep-inside response she felt to the sexy, generous man. The transition endangered her objectivity. Far worse, in the long run she feared it endangered her heart.

She was sitting in the therapy room stirring cream into her coffee when Carolanne came in and sank down in the chair across from her.

"What a day," the other therapist declared wearily. "It's days like this that make me wish I sold little cones of frozen yogurt for a living. No stress. No life-or-death crisis. No temper tantrums."

"Obviously you've never been around a three-year-old whose cone just upended on the ground."

"It couldn't possibly be any worse than this," she said fervently, then turned her full attention on Jenny. "Come to think of it, you don't look so perky yourself. Even your curls have lost their bounce. What's the story, or need I ask? What's the gorgeous Frank Chambers done now?"

"He invited me to play strip poker."

Carolanne's eyes danced with amusement. "Well, well, that is progress. Talk about incentives to get those hands working again. You've obviously inspired him. You should be proud."

"Proud? The man terrifies me."

"Because you're responding to him, right? So what's the big deal? It's about time you let yourself fall in love again."

"Who said anything about falling in love? All I mentioned was a sneaky attempt to get my clothes off."

"A man like that would not strip you naked in a hospital room unless his intentions were very serious."

Jenny groaned and put her head down on her arms. "This isn't happening."

"What isn't happening?"

"Frank Chambers is not interested in me and I am definitely not interested in him."

Carolanne nodded slowly. "Okay. I think I get it. Nothing's happening between the two of you, so there's no reason for you to go crazy, right?"

"Right."

"Then why have you added cream to a cup of cold water?"

Jenny glanced down and saw the murky white liquid in the coffee cup. "Oh, dear Lord."

"*He* might give you an answer," Carolanne said. "But there's someone a lot closer who could really clear things up."

"Who?"

"Frank Chambers."

"He can't clear anything up. He's the problem."

"Why?"

"If I knew that, there wouldn't be a problem."

Carolanne looked more bewildered than ever. "One of us in this room is going to be in need of psychiatric counseling very shortly, and something tells me it's going to be me unless you start talking plain English."

Jenny drew in a deep breath. "All patients tend to form a bond with their therapist, true?"

"Yes."

"So what Frank thinks he feels for me is no more than a passing infatuation, right? Maybe mixed in with some gratitude?"

"That's not the look I saw in his eyes, but I'll go along with you for the sake of this conversation."

Jenny shot her a disgruntled look. "I should be used to that kind of reaction. It's never bothered me before."

Carolanne's expression suddenly brightened with understanding. "But it does this time, because you're falling for him."

"I am not!" Jenny's blurted denial echoed in the therapy room.

Her friend sighed. "If you say so, though why you're fighting it is beyond me. At least half a dozen nurses on the unit are taking bets on which one can win the man's heart, and he hasn't asked any of them to play strip poker. I'm going home to my simple, uncomplicated cat.''

Jenny mustered a faint smile. "There is nothing uncomplicated about Minx. She's as neurotic as the rest of us."

"Speak for yourself," Carolanne said, getting her purse from her locker. She paused at the door. "Call if you need me, okay?"

"Sure. Thanks for listening."

When the other therapist had gone, Jenny tried to concentrate on some of the supervisory paperwork entailed in the job, the paperwork she couldn't seem to get done when Frank was in the room. She couldn't work up any enthusiasm for it now, either. An hour later, tired of fighting the inevitable, she headed back down the hall to Room 407.

Outside Frank's door, she could hear the deep rumble of conversation, the frequent bursts of laughter. Opening the door a crack, she peered inside and saw that he was once again surrounded by family. One of the men, a little shorter and stockier than Frank but unmistakably a Chambers, was holding up a handful of paint chips. It had to be Jared, she thought, grinning at the sight of all those shades of blue.

Just as she was about to let the door drift closed, Frank looked up, his gaze locking with hers. That jolt of awareness that came each time their eyes met shot through her. Her knees nearly buckled with the shock of it.

"Hey," he called softly. "Come on in. You're the one who got me into this. You have to choose."

Half a dozen pairs of fascinated eyes immediately turned to her. Jenny tried to ignore the not-so-subtle exchange of glances—from Jared to Frank to Tim to Karyn and yet more of the Chambers brothers she had yet to meet. The family resemblance was obvious, though.

As if they'd sensed her discomfort, every one of the brothers began to talk at once, spurred by Karyn's blatant attempt to distract them with what was clearly a familiar family argument. In the midst of the chaotic babble, Jenny's gaze sought Frank's again. The look in his eyes drew her closer. "Sit here," he said, sliding over on the bed until there was room on the edge.

Seated next to him, hip to hip, her pulse skittered wildly. He held out the dozen or so paint chips. "What do you think?"

The shades ranged from vivid royal blue to palest turquoise, from chalky Wedgewood to deepest azure. The one that drew her, though, was the clear blue tint that matched Frank's eyes.

"This one," she said at once, suddenly oblivious to the crowd of fascinated onlookers. She was surprised when a heated debate erupted over the choice.

"Why that one?" Tim demanded.

"I'll bet I know," Karyn said, meeting Jenny's gaze with a look of instinctive feminine understanding.

Jenny found herself grinning despite the risk of embarrassment. "I'll bet you do, too."

"Why?" came the masculine chorus.

"Never mind," Karyn said briskly, giving Jenny's hand a warm squeeze. "Let's get out of Frank's hair, you guys. I think he's due for another therapy session."

"At this hour?" Jared said, then blinked rapidly at a forceful nudge from his sister. "Oh, yeah. Just like the other night. Let's go, guys."

"Pretty intuitive bunch," Frank said when they'd swarmed out. "Is that what you had in mind, a little therapy?"

Jenny shook her head. "I'm not sure what I had in mind."

"Maybe an apology?"

Her defenses slammed into place. "From me? I haven't done anything to apologize for."

"No, but I have. I guess I didn't realize that you were really worried about Otis's gambling. I've been thinking about your reaction ever since you left here this afternoon. I'm sorry if I did anything to make it worse."

She shook her head, weariness settling in. "I shouldn't blame you. I can't run his life for him. All I can do is encourage him to get help if it gets out of hand. I have a hunch he makes it sound a whole lot worse than it is just to bug me."

"Has he ever borrowed money from you?"

"A few dollars before payday, but he's always paid it back. Other people around here have given him loans, too." She stood up and began to pace. "He's not a deadbeat, though. I don't think he's really in debt to anybody. If it were just a form of entertainment like going to the movies, I wouldn't worry so, but he seems a little compulsive about it."

"And I took advantage of that just to keep from being bored. It won't happen again."

"Thanks."

His gaze fastened on her. "So if you didn't stop by to drag an apology out of me, why did you come?"

"Must be your charming company." She tossed the words out casually, but she sensed that her nervous pacing of the room betrayed her. Frank seemed to see right through her.

"Want to tell me what's really on your mind?" he said quietly. He moved to where she stood by the window.

She wondered what he'd do if she simply blurted out that he was affecting her deeply in a way that made her long for things she'd nearly forgotten: love, family, companionship, romance. Not that she was likely to make that kind of an admission and damage their professional rapport.

"Maybe this?" he suggested, leaning close to brush his lips across hers.

The kiss was no more than the whisper of butterfly wings, but it rocked her. When his arms clumsily drew her closer, she stiffened, then relaxed into the wonderful sensation. His lips covered hers again and this time there was nothing sweet or innocent about the touch. It was all heat and hunger and claiming. If the first had been a gentle spring rain, this was all lightning and thunder. Just when she felt as if the world might be spinning off its axis, buffeted by the power-ful force of that kiss, he pulled back.

"Of course, I could be wrong," he said in a voice that was meant to be light, but seemed somehow choked. The blue of his eyes was shades darker than the color she'd matched only moments before.

Jenny couldn't seem to catch her breath or to form a single sensible thought. She was still caught up in the taste and feel of that potent kiss.

"We could always play poker," he teased, when she remained silent.

She finally found her voice and even managed a lit-tle feigned indignation. "Forget it. I hid the cards."

"If you really want to stick around, we could watch TV."

That struck her as innocuous enough. "Okay."

Frank moved back to the bed and hit the remote control to turn it on. "There's room next to me, if you'd care to snuggle up."

That kiss made her cautious. She grinned and pulled up the chair. "Don't press your luck."

"Too bad there's no popcorn. What's a movie date without popcorn?"

The cozy image was too appealing to ignore. "I could go get some from the vending machine and put it in the microwave."

"Do you want some, too?"

She thought about it and nodded. "Yes, as a mat-ter of fact. I'm starved."

It wasn't until she'd come back with the popcorn and the sodas that she realized exactly how devious

Frank's suggestion really was. The only way he could eat the buttery kernels was if she sat next to him on the bed and fed them to him.

"You're a sneak," she accused as she perched uneasily by his side. "And don't turn that innocent look on me. You're about as innocent as Don Juan."

"You didn't have to share the popcorn," he argued.

"Sure. I could have stayed in the chair, munched away and watched you pout."

"You wouldn't have done that."

"You think you know me pretty well, don't you?"

"Well enough."

"And?"

"I think you've finally decided to stop fighting me."

Jenny sighed and gave herself up to the unfamiliar feeling of contentment that was stealing over her, to the memory of that intense kiss. "Just for tonight."

For once, Frank didn't argue with her. "That's a start, sweetheart. That's a start."

Six

Frank felt as if he'd been sucker-punched. After days of progress, after days of focusing more intently on Jenny then on his own situation, he suddenly slammed into reality. The bandages were off for good, the skin healed over sufficiently to avoid the danger of infection. He stared at his badly scarred hands as if they belonged to someone else.

Sure, he'd glimpsed them during other dressing changes, but somehow he'd been expecting an improvement, some miracle that would cause the scars to vanish overnight. Now Dr. Wilding was telling him matter-of-factly that wouldn't happen, that the redness would fade eventually, but the scarring was permanent. He tried to imagine spending the rest of his life with this kind of disfigurement. He'd thought it wouldn't bother him. Now his stomach churned at the prospect.

"Not bad," the doctor murmured in satisfaction. "You can think about plastic surgery, skin grafting, if you like, but I don't think you'll see much improvement over this or I would have recommended it sooner. You're lucky, young man. It could have been worse."

Lucky? What was lucky about having hands that ought to be covered with gloves around the clock? He tried to remind himself of the way they'd looked before, of the nicks and cuts, the calluses that had made his work-roughened hands anything but picture perfect. Even that had been a hell of an improvement on this.

Frank finally tore his gaze away from the fresh scars and dared to meet Jenny's eyes. His whole body tensed as he waited for some faint sign of repulsion.

She was frowning, her lower lip caught between her teeth, but he'd come to realize over the past few days that she did that often, whenever she was worried or deep in thought. Slowly her lips curved into a familiar reassuring smile. It reached all the way to her incredible eyes, but Frank wasn't convinced. Doubts very nearly overwhelmed him. What woman would ever want hands like this touching her? He tried to imagine the tight red skin against the perfect pale silk of Jenny's breasts, the curve of her hip, but his imagination failed him.

The anger of those first awful days, the doubts he'd had before about his professional future, were nothing compared to the agonizing emptiness that now stole into his soul. He would never know the sweetness of an intimate moment like that, never to allow himself to sully her perfect beauty with his ugliness.

There was a bitter irony to discovering a woman he could love, only to realize that a relationship between them could never happen. Gentle, tenderhearted Jenny was filled with compassion, not just for him but for the entire world. He'd seen it in the way she cared for her other patients, in the way she worried about Otis. It was sweet temptation to let himself bask in that warmth, to accept her pity and call it love.

He couldn't do it. Filled with a raging anger at the injustice, he vowed he wouldn't. He steeled himself against all the longings that had been building for the past days. It would take every bit of his strength not to act on the desire that teased his senses whenever she was near. That one deep, drugging kiss they had shared the night before would never be repeated, not if he could help it. The minute those discharge papers were signed, he'd walk out of this hospital and out of her life.

As the last days of his hospital stay passed, Jenny knew exactly what was going through Frank's mind. She'd seen it all before. She recognized that gut-deep uncertainty that had him shouting at everyone within range again. The reaction might be typical, but in Frank it was magnified a thousand times because of the kind of man he was. Used to creating flawless beauty, he was being forced to come to grips with imperfection. It might be superficial and unimportant in her eyes or anyone else's, but to his artistic view that first this-is-it view of his burn-scarred hands must have seemed devastating.

After that one instant of raw anguish she'd read in his eyes when the bandages had come off for good, he'd shut himself off from her—maybe even from himself. For the past three days he had come into the therapy room on schedule, but he'd barely spoken. Today was more of the same.

He sat now, his back rigid, doing his exercises with ferocious intensity, oblivious to the beads of sweat forming on his brow, ignoring the tension that was evident in the powerful muscles across his shoulders. When she could stand it no longer, she pulled out the chair next to his and sat. Her heart aching for him, with one hand she reached over and stilled his.

"Enough," she said.

The quiet order brought his head up, his combative gaze clashing with hers. She sensed he was about to argue, but then his gaze slid away. He slowly and deliberately withdrew his hands and hid them beneath the table, his emotional and physical retreat complete.

"No," she insisted and held out her hand. "Please don't ever hide from me. Don't hide from anyone."

As she waited, she could hear each tick of the clock as its big hands clicked off the passing minutes. Finally, an eternity later, Frank put his hands back on the table. Jenny took the right one in hers and gently stroked the marred skin. The muscles in his forearm jerked, then stilled. His jaw clenched, but this time he didn't draw away from her. Nor did he look at her.

"Such wonderful, powerful hands," she murmured. "I've been to see your work, you know. I've never seen anything so beautiful."

"That's over now," he said, his expression bleak.

"You know better than that," she said impatiently. "You've had a temporary setback because of the fire, that's all. You'll work again. You're improving every day. Can't you see that?"

He shrugged with clearly feigned indifference. "Maybe. Maybe not."

She studied him, the way he avoided looking at her, the way he glanced at his hands—and hers—then at the floor, his dismay evident. "You're worried about how the scars look, aren't you?" When he started to shake his head in denial, she stopped him. "No. Don't even try to deny that little bit of vanity. It's perfectly natural."

He regarded her with angry astonishment. "You think this is about something as trivial as my vanity?"

"Isn't it? We're the sum of all our parts, you know, not any one. Yet we have a way of focusing totally on what we perceive as our flaws."

She watched him closely, trying to gauge his reaction. His eyes were shuttered. "Have you ever noticed that?" she prodded. "We're the first to mention an imperfection in ourselves, to draw attention to it, joke about it, just to let everyone know we're aware of it, just to get in the first critical remark. You've heard women joke about their thighs or men kid about their baldness. They want the world to know it doesn't matter to them, when what they're really proving is that it does matter terribly... to them.''

Frank listened attentively, but his expression remained skeptical. Not even her touch seemed to reassure him. She tried again to coax him out of his self-pity.

''If you let the scars become important to you, then they'll be important to everyone you know. Accept them, Frank. Accept them, just the way you do the color of your eyes and the beat of your heart. They're a part of a man who's very special.''

As she spoke she could feel her throat clog with emotions she rarely allowed herself. Her words had a too familiar ring, dredging up old hurts, old emotions she had thought long buried. A tear clung to her lashes, then spilled down her cheek. When the dampness fell onto Frank's hand, he lifted a startled gaze to meet hers. Whatever he was feeling, though, he covered it, as usual, with anger.

''What the hell do you know about it?'' he demanded roughly. ''Is this lesson number ten on the road to recovery? It's all so pat. You're good, Jenny. I'll give you that. You almost had me believing you. The tears did it. Did you major in therapy and minor in acting?''

This time she was the one jerking away. This time she was the one who could feel the fury building up like the winds of a hurricane. "Damn you!"

"Someone beat you to it. I've already been damned. I look at these hands and all I see is the ugliness, all I feel is the pain. How can you even bear to touch them?"

"What you feel is self-pity, you arrogant, self-centered jerk!"

For the first time in her career, Jenny allowed her fury to overrule her professional demeanor. It felt wonderful. She couldn't have banked the anger now if her entire career had depended on it. Emotions that had little to do with Frank and much to do with her own tattered pride came pouring out.

"Do you think you're the only person ever to be badly scarred? Do you?" she demanded. "There are a dozen patients in the unit right now who are worse off than you. Some will have hideous facial scars that no amount of surgery will fix. Some will be lucky to survive at all."

He waved a hand dismissively. "I'm not talking about them. I know that compared to them I'm damned fortunate. I look at Pam and it makes me sick to think what she'll go through. Right now, though, I'm talking about you. Where do you get off telling me or any one of the others how to feel, how to live our lives and accept ourselves? I'm sick of the platitudes, sick of the condescension."

She stared at him in astonishment. "Condescension? You think that's what this is all about? Damn

you, Frank Chambers hasn't it ever occurred to you
that I could know exactly how you feel? *Exactly!*
Maybe my scars aren't visible, but they're there.''

He opened his mouth, but she cut him off, her out-
rage unmistakable. ''You listen to me for once,'' she
insisted. She sucked in a deep breath, then said more
quietly, ''When they cut off my breast to rid me of
cancer, they left me with an ugly gash across my chest.
Oh, the surgeon was good enough. He prettied it up
with neat stitches, but there's no mistaking that kind
of wound. You try telling me, telling any woman that
losing a breast doesn't matter. Try telling us we're still
whole. We won't believe you. Every swimsuit ad,
every television commercial, says otherwise. We know
what feminine beauty is all about.''

She was barely aware of Frank's sudden indrawn
breath, the tenderness that instantly replaced cold fury
in his eyes.

''Don't you get it?'' she asked him. ''We can only
learn to live again when we can say it to ourselves,
when somewhere deep inside we do believe that we're
whole and attractive despite the scars. So, don't you
act like some macho jerk because your hands aren't
pretty. You'll live, dammit, and in the end that's the
only thing that matters.''

''I'm sorry,'' Frank whispered, his voice ragged. He
was shaken to the very depths of his being by Jenny's
astonishing tirade and even more unexpected revelation. When she turned away, when she would have
run, he grabbed her, oblivious to his own pain, tor-

mented by hers and the inadvertent way he'd added to
it.

"Don't you know how beautiful you are?" he said,
holding her. He raised his fingers to her cheek, hesitated, then forced himself to caress the silken curve of
her jaw, knowing as he did so that from this moment
on he would be lost. There would be no turning back
now from the love he felt for her, from his need to
protect and cherish her. He wouldn't be able to make
the noble sacrifice of walking away, not when she was
filled with so much pain, so many doubts of her own.
"Don't you know how proud any man would be to be
with you?"

A deep sigh shuddered through her, but still she
wouldn't look at him. Her gaze was fixed firmly on the
floor as if there were something in the pattern of the
tiles more fascinating than anything he could possibly
say.

"Jenny, I'm sorry. I'm sorry for being such a fool."

She sighed heavily and her arms slid around his
waist. She pressed her cheek, damp with tears, against
his chest. "You don't get condemned to hell for being
a fool," she muttered finally.

"Maybe not by God," he agreed. "How about by
you?"

She lifted her head then, very slowly. More tears had
welled in her eyes and were spilling down her cheeks.
"I've never condemned you for hurting, Frank. I've
just wanted to make it stop. I've just wanted you to
know that I understood what you're going through.
It's not easy picking up the pieces and going on when

life slams you with a setback like you've had, but you have to do it. Sooner or later, you have to let go of the anger and do whatever needs to be done."

"And have you done that?" he asked, certain that she hadn't been nearly as good at taking the advice as she was at dishing it out. "Have you let go of the anger?"

"Most of the time. Maybe it's easier for me, because I can hide the scar. I don't have to deal with it, not out loud."

He studied her closely and sensed that there was so much she wasn't saying, so much she might not even be admitting to herself. "But out loud isn't the hard part, is it?"

She gave him a wobbly smile. Like Pam's brave attempts, it shattered his heart.

"No," she admitted. "It's what happens deep inside in the middle of the night. That's when there's no stopping the doubts, no holding back the terror."

As Frank held her, he prayed she could feel the compassion surround her, strengthen her if only she'd let it. For some reason, though, he could tell she was holding back, refusing to take what he was offering.

"Have you been with a man since the surgery?" he asked out of the blue, guessing suddenly at the real reason for her torment. Some fool had fed her doubts, had failed to offer the reassuring touch that she had just offered him. His voice was gentle, but from her instantaneous transformation, he saw that the question ripped through her defenses and opened old wounds. Jenny reacted to the raw pain with instantly renewed fury.

"How dare you ask me that? Have you forgotten what our relationship is? It's professional. I'm a therapist. You're my patient. No more. That doesn't entitle you to pry into my personal life."

"You opened the door. From the first day you walked into my room, we've both known there was something more between us, something we couldn't walk away from if we tried."

"No," she denied too quickly. She raised her hands as if to ward off any further painful intrusions. "You're wrong."

Backing away from him, from the emotions, she said, "I have to go. Dr. Wilding intends to discharge you in the morning. I'll try to come by before you leave."

But she didn't come by. Frank waited, watching the door all morning. When he could stand it no longer, he left his room and walked down the hall to the therapy room. Otis was standing just outside the door.

"Hear you're going home today," the orderly said. "How am I supposed to win any money with you gone?"

"I'm afraid my gambling days are over."

"So she got you, too?" he asked with a chuckle. "That woman thinks she can save the whole wide world. She's got a good heart." Eyes the color of melted chocolate watched Frank's reaction. "You ain't mistaking tnat for something else, are you?"

Frank shook his head. What he felt for Jenny was no mistake. What she felt for him was just as powerful. He had to convince her of that. He had to apologize, though, for the way he'd intruded so crudely into her personal life last night, asking questions that he hadn't led up to first with flowers and sweet words to prove how much he cared. He had to show her that there was no need for secrets between them. He had to know if some foolish man had shattered her fragile self-esteem with a careless remark, a flicker of revulsion at the sight of her scars. He would spend the rest of his life making that up to her, proving that she was all woman, both inside and out.

"Is she in there now? I need to see her."

"She's with a patient." He didn't move an inch, his body blocking the door.

Frank's gaze narrowed. "Otis, did she say something to you about me?"

The orderly's expression remained perfectly bland, but there was no mistaking the streak of protectiveness in his stance. "Is there something to say?" he countered.

Frank sighed. "No. Nothing. Tell her I'll be in my room another hour or so. Kevin's picking me up on his lunch hour."

Jenny had recognized what was happening with Frank even before last night. Hell, she and Carolanne had even talked about it. She'd had patients think they were in love with her before. She'd blithely ignored their protestations, knowing that as soon as the link of therapy was broken, they would resume their old lives. They had. And once Frank left today, he would be no different.

Except in her heart. Something about the wonderful, foul-tempered beast had gotten to her. He had so much love to give. He was a living monument to the theory that the more love you gave, the more you had to give. She'd never met a man who had more people relying on him and who thrived on it so.

For nearly two weeks now she'd been on the fringes of all that love and loyalty, and she'd felt like a kid with her nose pressed to the window of a toy store. But as much as she'd come to care for Frank, as recklessly as she'd indulged in her fantasies about sharing the warmth of his family, a life for the two of them simply wasn't in the cards. Once he'd coped with his own scars, she wouldn't burden him with hers.

She hadn't planned to tell him as much as she had about the breast cancer. It wasn't something she hid from her friends, but it certainly wasn't relevant to their patient-therapist relationship. At least it never had been with any other patient. If they'd thought her compassion deeper than most of the staff's, they'd never seemed to wonder why. With Frank, though, a lot of things about that professional relationship were shifting like sands at the whim of an angry tide.

She was standing just inside the door of the therapy room when she thought she heard his voice. She could hear Otis's mellow tones countering Frank's. Her heart climbed up to her throat and seemed to lodge there. When it was finally silent again in the hallway, she peeked out.

"He's gone," Otis said dryly, "though why you'd want to be avoiding him is beyond me. I ain't seen a man so far gone over a woman in a long time."

"I think the psychological term is transference."

"Funny, I thought it was lust."

She glowered at him. "You can leave now, Otis."

"I've done my part, so you don't need to listen to what I have to say? I don't think so," he said, backing her into the room, his big hands shooing her toward a chair. "You sit for just a minute, miss, and let me tell you what I see here."

"Otis!" she warned.

"Don't you go all prim and proper on me. You and me, we've always understood each other, from the day I wheeled you down the hall to surgery and back again. You held this hand of mine and spilled your guts, so I guess I've got a pretty good idea what's on your mind now."

"Otis, I really don't want to talk about this," Jenny said.

"That's okay by me. You can just listen. That's a fine man who just left here. Any man who's got the love of a family the way he does has done something special to deserve it. You'd do well to hang on to him. If you don't, that's up to you. The way I've got it figured, though, you owe him."

She opened her mouth to argue, but he kept right on lecturing. "You're the one who single handedly gave him the will to fight. You abandon him now, he just might give up, and we both know he's a long way from being recovered. Now you can send Carolanne or one of the others over there to help him settle in at home, and you can assign one of them to work with him when he comes in as an outpatient, but that's the coward's way out. Maybe I'm wrong, but I don't think you're a coward.''

He waited a beat, his gaze expectant. Jenny could feel her cheeks turn pink. Satisfied with her embarrassed reaction, Otis nodded. "I guess I've said my piece. You think about it." He turned on his heel and walked out, leaving her with more to think about than he could possibly imagine.

"But I *am* a coward," she whispered to his retreating back. She wasn't just running from Frank. She wasn't simply afraid of loving.

She was terrified she wouldn't be around long enough to make it last.

In her heart, she knew Otis was right. She couldn't abandon Frank now. If it took every ounce of courage she possessed, she would see this through to the end.

Seven

———

Frank stood in the doorway of his private wood-working shop at home, unable to tear his gaze away from two intricately carved, skillfully crafted cabinets in unfinished cherry and oak. He rarely did his cabinetry at home, but these had been special orders and he'd spent his spare time rushing to complete them. His dedication had saved them from the fire. He wondered, though, if they would ever be finished, if the twining flowers along the edges would ever reach as high as he'd intended.

His gaze moved on to the smaller, partially carved blocks of wood that sat amid the fragrant shavings on top of his worktable. Smooth, polished pieces, ready for summer gallery showing, lined a shelf along one wall. Each one was a triumph of his artistic imagination over nature. It wasn't until he'd studied the grain of the wood that he decided what shape it would take. It was as if each square or rectangular block spoke to his mind's eye. Stepping inside, he slowly approached the complete figures, his heart aching at the prospect of never again being able to create such beauty.

He'd heard it said that the first step in any difficult task was always the hardest, and this one had been pure hell. It had taken him days just to work up the courage to come this far. He'd insisted that Kevin shut the door to the back room the day he'd come home from the hospital. He'd skirted the room ever since, not even glancing at the closed door when he could avoid it. He'd spent the days going for walks. Long, exhausting walks. Nights, he'd lain in bed and thought of Jenny and a future that seemed even emptier without her. It was still impossible for him to accept that she hadn't come, that she'd meant it when she'd said there could be nothing between them. And he thought of the painful revelation that, to her way of thinking, might have made it impossible for her to come. He drifted to sleep eventually filled with terrible questions.

When he'd awakened late this morning, he'd known he could no longer put off the inevitable. He had to know just how bleak the future was, just how crippling his injury had been. Once he knew that, maybe he'd know what to do about Jenny as well, whether he dared to pursue her, whether he'd have the strength to help her face her own demons.

Now that he was inside the room with happier memories crowding in, risking it seemed like a lousy idea. Maybe it would be better not to know just how terribly inept his fingers had become. Maybe he should just accept that fate had intervened and set his life on a different course. But what course? What the hell would he do with the rest of his life if not this?

For years, beginning at the age of seventeen, he had taken safe, low-paying, unskilled jobs to help out at home. Only when his extra income was no longer needed had he dared to begin the uncertain career that had beckoned to him from the first time he'd held a stick of wood and been taught whittling by his Tennessee-born father. From the first day of his apprenticeship to a master craftsman, he'd been filled with a soul-deep sense of accomplishment. What if all that was truly over? How would he handle it? Could he go back to those other less challenging, less satisfying jobs?

Finally, when he could bear it no more, he reached for one of the unfinished pieces. Gritting his teeth against the pain, aware of the tautness of his skin as it stretched almost beyond endurance, he closed his hand around the chunky block. With an artist's tender touch, he rubbed his still raw fingertips over the wood, stroking it as if it were alive, caressing the rounded shape of a blue jay's belly as it emerged from the uneven surface.

There were those who said that it was possible to distinguish each fragile feather on figures he'd carved. On this piece he had yet to complete the basic carving, much less start the delicate detail. Fingers trembling, he reached for his knife. Slowly, painfully, he closed his hand around it, defying Jenny's warning not to rush his attempts to hold smaller objects, not to allow his expectations to soar too high. With grim determination, he touched knife to wood, only to have the sharp instrument slide from his feeble grasp.

With a muttered oath, he picked it up and tried again, ignoring the agony, ignoring the sting of perspiration that beaded across his brow and trickled into his eyes, ignoring the sick churning of fear in his belly. Again, the knife clattered to the floor.

With each faulty effort, with each demoralizing defeat, his determination wavered, but he tried again... and again. Sweat ran down his back. His arms and shoulders ached from the effort of trying to master no more than a firm hold on what had once seemed a natural extension of his body.

It was on his tenth try or his thirtieth—he had lost track—when he heard the whisper of sound. He turned to find Jenny standing in the doorway, her face streaked with sympathetic tears. The leaden mass that had formed in his chest grew heavier still at the sight of her brokenhearted expression.

"How'd you get in?" he asked dully, his shoulders slumping.

"I knocked. I guess you didn't hear me. I tried the door and it was open." With her distraught gaze fixed on his hands, she said, "You shouldn't be doing this. It's too soon."

"I had to try. I had to know the worst."

Something that looked like guilt flickered in her eyes. "I should have been here," she said, almost to herself. Her gaze rose, then met his. "You're my patient. I should have come the first day you missed your outpatient appointment."

"Why didn't you?" he asked accusingly.

"It just seemed so complicated. I kept thinking you would come back to the hospital. Today, when you missed the second appointment, I knew there was no choice. I had to come."

The weight of her guilt got to him. "Don't go blaming yourself," he said, feeling a twinge of guilt himself. Had he known that staying away would bring her to him? Maybe so. Maybe the real blame was his. He said only, "I knew the risk I was taking by not continuing the therapy. I figured a few days off couldn't matter all that much."

"A few days?" she questioned. "Or were you really giving up?"

He shook his head. "Not until today."

Tears welled again in her eyes, but she blinked them away. "I won't let you do that, Frank."

Those tears were going to be his undoing. "Don't cry," he pleaded, his own voice ragged with emotion as he found himself offering comfort to a woman whose slightest smile had come to mean comfort to him. He yearned to take her in his arms, to touch her as he had no right to touch her, to show her what she'd come to mean to him.

She started to speak again, then shook her head.

"What the hell," he said with pure bravado, hoping to win a smile, an end to the unbearable tension throbbing between them. "I can always hold the handle of a saw. Maybe I can build houses."

"You will carve again," she vowed. "I promise."

Grateful beyond belief that she had come at last, Frank was still in no mood for promises that might never be kept. In a gesture of pure defiance, he swept his arm across the worktable, sending wood and tools flying. "No, dammit! Don't lie to me, Jenny. Never lie to me. Let me adjust. Let me get on with my life."

A familiar mutinous expression settled on her lips, firmed her jaw. She swiped away the tears. "What kind of a life will it be, if you can't do what you love?" she demanded. "You can't stop trying."

"I can," he said, just as stubbornly. "And I will."

She sucked in a breath and stood straighter, every inch filled with that magnificent indignation that could have daunted kings or generals. He was no match at all when she declared, "I won't let you."

Frank's laugh was mirthless, just the same. "Jenny, there's not a blessed thing you can do about it," he mocked.

As if he'd thrown down a gauntlet in some medieval challenge, she marched into the room. "Watch me," she said, picking up the first tool she came to and slapping the handle into his hand. "Squeeze it, damn you."

Raw pain seared his flesh, but by instinct his fingers curved around the instrument, the skin stretched taut, the nerve endings on fire.

"Tighter," she demanded, her body pressed against him in a way that had him thinking of things far softer than oak, far more compelling than carving. The force of the desire spiraling through him shook him to the very core of his being.

Their gazes clashed, hers filled with furious determination, his own filled with God knew what revelation. When the knife threatened to slide from his grasp again, she folded her own hand around his, adding enough pressure to secure it. Every muscle in Frank's body tensed at this new and very difficult strain, but he refused to let go, refused to acknowledge the agony of the effort. Jenny was clearly willing to goad him into trying, and he was too stubborn and too proud not to accept the challenge. Nor could he bear the thought of her moving away. God help him, he wouldn't deny himself the sweet, sweet pleasure of her nearness.

"You know the drill," she said finally, her voice oddly breathless. "Ten minutes an hour."

"Who's going to be around to make me?"

"I am."

"Your job as my therapist ended when I walked out of the hospital."

Green eyes sparked with emerald fire. "Like hell. A condition of your discharge was that you continue therapy as an outpatient. If I hadn't come today, Dr. Wilding would have sent me over to find out where the hell you've been."

Despite himself, Frank's lips twitched with amusement. A whisper of relief sighed through him, and he felt himself begin to relax. "Think you're pretty tough, don't you?"

That earned a dimpled smile that faded quickly into a clearly feigned scowl. "You bet," she declared.

"And if I don't cooperate?"

"You don't want to know what kind of tortures I can invent for an uncooperative patient."

He chuckled, fully aware of the kind of tortures she could impose without even trying. His body ached from them. "Is that so?" he taunted. His gaze fastened on the lush curve of her lips.

"Care to test me?" she taunted right back.

"Lady, I intend to give you a run for your money." He winked as he said it, suddenly feeling better, more hopeful, even if hope was folly. "By the way, what do I get if I cooperate?"

"You get to work again."

"I had something a little more intimate in mind."

"I'll just bet you did," she retorted. As if suddenly aware of the way her body had molded itself to him, she backed away, a step only, but it was too far for him. Frank wanted to curse at the sudden deprivation.

"You finish that blue jay and then maybe we'll talk," she said.

"Talking is the last thing on my mind," he said bluntly so there could be no doubts about his intentions.

A blush crept into her cheeks, but her eyes were stormy. Hands on slender hips, she said, "Mister, if your hands heal half as well as your libido, you'll be in great shape in no time."

At the sound of a deep-throated chuckle, they both whirled around to see Tim lurking in the doorway. Amusement danced in his eyes. "Hey, Bro, what's this about a libido? I thought I had the reputation in the family for chasing skirts."

Disgruntled by the untimely interruption, Frank said, "Listen, *Bro,* you're interrupting my therapy."

"Oh, is that what this is? Where can I sign up?" He winked at Jenny, and the brazen little hussy winked back. Frank wanted to throttle them both as the charged atmosphere disintegrated. Another few seconds of sparring, another half dozen words of challenge and Jenny would have been in his arms, maybe even in his lonely king-size bed just down the hall. A betting man—Otis—could have made book on it.

"If you don't get out of here in the next ten seconds, your broken arm will qualify you," Frank said grumpily.

Jenny shook her head. "Okay, enough, you two. I'm out of here. Play nice."

Tim's eyes widened at the teasing admonition. "You sound just like Ma."

"Is it any wonder, when you sound like a couple of five-year-olds?" She turned her very best, most intimidating therapist-to-patient glare on Frank. "And you, ten minutes every hour. Got it?"

"Have you ever thought of a career in the military?" he inquired.

"Why, when I have guys like you to order around already? Be at the clinic tomorrow. Bring your tools with you. We might as well work with the things that are relevant to you."

"Why not have the sessions here?"

There was no arguing the logic of the suggestion, but Jenny's instantly terrified expression spoke volumes. She wasn't about to spend an hour a day with him in his home, where they both knew that therapy would take second place to mounting desire.

"Policy," she said tightly, her tone daring him to contradict her.

Much as he wanted to, suddenly Frank didn't have the stamina for it. The previous hour had stolen the last of his reserves of energy.

"I'll be there," he said.

When she nodded, secure again in the victory, he added, "But don't think you're one bit safer there, Jenny."

Patches of pink colored her cheeks for the second time in minutes. Avoiding Tim's laughing gaze and Frank's challenge, she scooted to safety.

Only when she had sashayed out of the room, the determined picture of feigned self-confidence, did Frank collapse onto his workbench. He was exhausted with the strain of coming into this room, of confronting his frailty all over again. The swing of his emotions from hope to defeat and back again had taken its toll.

Tim's expression immediately turned worried. "You okay?"

"Just a little tired."

"From the therapy, or from the stress of keeping your hands off the therapist?"

Frank grinned ruefully. "The only interest the therapist has in my hands is their increasing manual dexterity."

"Sounds promising."

"Very funny."

Tim's expression sobered. "What about you? You're really attracted to her, aren't you?

"What's not to like? She's beautiful. She's bright. She's caring. She's gentle. She's sexy. And all she feels for me is pity." He said the last as a diversion, praying it wasn't entirely true, unwilling to admit it might be.

"I don't think so."

"You didn't see the look on her face when she walked in here an hour ago."

"Did it ever occur to you that maybe it was compassion, not pity? Jenny strikes me as a woman who feels things deeply. Maybe what she was feeling was the ache inside you. Anyone who knows you can see what kind of hell you're going through."

Frank prayed that Tim was right, that his own instincts about Jenny's susceptibility to him were equally on target. He regarded his brother curiously. "You know something, little brother? I think maybe I've been selling you short all these years. Under all that flirtatious, chauvinistic attitude beats the heart of a true romantic. I predict that once you truly fall for a woman, it's going to be a crash heard round the entire Bay area.''

"God, I hope not. We have enough quakes as it is.''

Jenny discovered that just because Frank was on her turf, just because he'd agreed to continue the therapy at the hospital's outpatient clinic, it didn't stop the lingering looks. Every time their fingers brushed, her whole body came alive. It was the most amazing reaction. She would have sworn that his were the damaged nerves, yet she felt as if it were her own that were healing. Contact meant only to guide took on a deeper meaning. She began to long for those casual, innocent touches, needing them for the good they did her, rather than the comfort and guidance they gave him. It had been years since she'd allowed herself to hunger for that kind of physical closeness.

She was careful, though, to make sure that there were always other patients around. When the scheduling failed her, she begged Carolanne to stay in the therapy room to finish paperwork.

"What are you afraid of?'' Carolanne demanded. "Frank Chambers is getting too close, isn't he? He's tearing down that wall of reserve, brick by brick.''

"That's about it.''

"What's so terrible about that?''

"Yeah,'' an all-too-familiar voice echoed. "What's so terrible about that? I'm a nice guy.''

With a fiery blush creeping up her neck, she turned to meet Frank's laughing eyes. Carolanne made a beeline for the door. "Traitor," Jenny muttered as her so-called friend left.

When Carolanne had gone, she bustled around the therapy room, giving orders, avoiding Frank's gaze, ignoring the thudding of her heart, the quick flare of heat deep inside.

"What'd you do last night?" he inquired casually as he dutifully began his exercises.

She blinked up from the paperwork she was pretending to read and stared at him. He didn't usually ask personal questions. "What?"

"I asked what you did last night."

"Why?"

He grinned. "What's the problem? That's a fairly typical question among friends. Fits right in there with 'Hi, how are you?' So, what did you do?"

She had to search her brain to recall what had filled the lonely hours until sleep had claimed her. "I read a paper on the importance of infection control in burn therapy."

"Sounds dull," he said, but he looked smug for some reason that eluded her.

"Actually it was fascinating." She launched into a desperate detailing of every word she could remember. She was only sorry the paper had been so short. More of the medical jargon might have dampened the unmistakable gleam she saw in his eyes.

"Still sounds dull," he said when she'd finished. "How come you didn't have a date?"

"Why the sudden interest in my social life?"

"I've always been interested in your social life. I've just never asked about it before."

"Why now?"

"Just scouting out the competition."

"There is no competition. You're not even in the running." The rapid clip of her pulse called her a liar.

So did the skeptical look in Frank's eyes. A lesser man would have been insulted. He apparently twisted the words to suit himself. "We'll see," he countered mildly.

Flustered, and determined not to let him see it, she moved to stand squarely in front of him and demanded, "Why are you doing this?"

"Doing what?"

"Trying to turn this into something personal. I can't continue working with you, if you insist on doing that. I'll have to turn you over to Carolanne."

"Hmm," he muttered thoughtfully. "That raises an interesting point."

"Which is?"

"If you're no longer my therapist, then you'd be free to go out with me. Am I interpreting this correctly?"

Jenny felt as if she were falling off the top of a very tall building with no net below. The sensation was heady but terrifying. "No. Absolutely not. That is not what I was saying at all," she sputtered with enough indignation to draw an unrepentant grin.

"You know what they say about ladies who protest too much."

Jenny might have slapped that smug expression right off his face, if she hadn't had just enough sense left to realize how he'd interpret that. "That's no protest, buddy," she said quietly. "That's a fact. You and I are patient and therapist or we are nothing. Is that clear enough for you?"

He smiled happily, which was not the reaction she'd been going for at all. "Very clear," he said cheerfully.

Why, if he was being so agreeable, did she have the feeling that she'd just lost a dangerous final round?

Eight

"I could really use some help from you in the kitchen," Frank mentioned casually to Jenny at the end of his third outpatient therapy session. "If you're not too busy, that is."

Jenny's instantly suspicious gaze shot to his. It was astonishing how deeply she distrusted his motives. Rightfully so, in this instance, he conceded ruefully.

"Meaning?" she said.

"I keep dropping those little microwave containers. Half the time my dinner ends up on the floor."

He made it sound as pitiful as possible, as if he were very likely to starve to death without assistance. The time had come to take drastic measures if he was going to get Jenny to begin trusting him outside the safety of the therapy room. For the time being, he wasn't going to worry about how trust might suffer when she discovered his sneaky, underhanded tactics.

"Couldn't your mother or Karyn help you out?" she suggested, a definite note of desperation in her voice. "Maybe your brothers could take turns."

Actually they had been doing exactly that, but Frank was not about to admit that to her. He didn't need their company. He needed hers. He needed the incredible lightness that his soul experienced when he was surrounded by her tenderness and optimism. He needed to give back to her some of the strength she'd shared with him. Most of all he needed the hot, urgent stirring of his blood that just being in the same room with her brought.

"Ma's been really good about bringing things over for dinner," he admitted. "It's getting them on the stove and then the table that's the problem. I don't want to tell her that, though. She'd just worry more than she already does. As for Karyn, she's left town with Brad while he preps for the Indy 500. She's a lousy cook anyway."

"That still leaves five brothers."

Fortunately Frank had anticipated all of her arguments and prepared. "Tim's working nights and he has his law classes all day. Jared's just started helping a neighbor paint his house. The others do what they can, but I want to be independent. I'm not used to having other people wait on me. If you could help me out a little, maybe fix up some gadgets so I could handle things better, I'd be able to make do on my own. A few more weeks and I should be past the worst of this, right?''

Suspicion darkened her eyes again. He could tell she was torn between that and the very real possibility that he hadn't had a decent dinner in days. ''I'll come by tonight,'' she said finally. ''About six?''

''Whatever's good for you. Consider it a treatment. Put it on my bill.''

She scowled at him. ''Don't be ridiculous.''

''No, really. I want this to be strictly professional. I don't want to take advantage of you. I know how you feel about me not stepping over that line.''

He sounded so noble, he couldn't imagine her not believing him. Even so, there was a long silence while she obviously continued to weigh his apparent sincerity against her doubts. ''You can share the dinner with me. That'll be payment enough,'' she said finally, though she was clearly unnerved by the prospect of sitting across from him at a dinner table. She was staring at the wall when she made the offer.

''That'd be great,'' he said with a shade too much enthusiasm. He quickly banked it, when her gaze shot back to him. ''I mean, if you have the time.''

''I do,'' she said curtly. ''Shall I pick up the groceries, or do you already have something you'd like me to fix?''

''Surprise me,'' he said, his gaze locking on hers. He lowered his voice to a seductive pitch. ''I really love surprises.''

''Frank,'' she began, her voice filled with renewed doubts.

"Yes?"

She sighed. "Never mind. I'll be there at six with the groceries."

"Reach in my pocket and grab my wallet," he suggested. "There should be enough in there for what you'll need from the store."

She looked every bit as panicky as if he'd blatantly suggested they make love in the linen closet down the hall. "This is my treat," she said hurriedly, taking a quick, revealing step back.

"No. I insist. How can it be your treat, if dinner is supposed to be my way of paying you back for cooking it?" He fixed his most innocent gaze on her. "My wallet's in the back pocket." He helpfully turned his backside to her.

Jenny complied with the enthusiasm of someone told they could have a million bucks as long as they didn't mind a few electrical shocks during the snatching of it. Only a seasoned pickpocket had the knack for removing a man's wallet without intimate contact. But for all her gifted hand gestures in therapy, Jenny was no pickpocket, and the photo-crammed wallet was a snug fit.

His breath caught in his throat as her hand slid nervously into his back pocket. Clumsiness turned the move into a lingering caress. Heat roared through him. Every nerve in his body throbbed in awareness. Even after Jenny had the wallet and was extracting a twenty-dollar bill, Frank trembled. If she was equally shaken, she hid it well, leaving him to wonder just who'd been the victor in this devious war of nerves.

Only when she glanced up and he saw the riot of emotions in her eyes did he declare the victory for himself. She shoved the wallet back in his pocket with so much force, he was surprised the denim didn't rip.

"I'll see you at six," she said and raced from the room.

Laughing, Frank went down the hall in search of Pam. Aware of the monotony of a long hospital stay, he'd been dropping by after his therapy sessions. He found her in her room with the TV on, but her face was turned toward the wall.

"Hey, beautiful, how are you?"

Instead of greeting him with her usual courageous, perky smile, the teenager kept her face averted. Then Frank noticed that the bandages on her head were gone. He swallowed hard against the tears that seemed to clog his throat at the sight of the red, scarred skin stretched taut over her cheekbone.

Drawing in a deep breath, he went around the bed and pulled up a chair. "Where's my smile?" he demanded, looking straight at her. "I thought you'd be glad to see me."

She tried to turn away again, but he touched her shoulder. "Don't," he said.

A tear slid down the unmarred side of her face. "But it's so awful," she whispered, pulling a pillow over her head. Her voice was muffled, but he could make out the rest of her heartbroken words. "I didn't know it was going to be like this. I'd seen the other patients, but I thought I'd be different."

Frank moved to the side of the bed, tugged the pillow gently away and forced her to face him. Then he opened his arms. With a sob, Pam launched herself at him and clung. "I'm never going to have any friends. Never. And I can't blame them. Who'd want to look at this?"

"I would," he said, his heart aching. "You know why? Because nothing that's important about you has changed. Inside, you're the same wonderful, funny, feisty girl you always were. You know what Jenny told me once?"

"What?"

"She said that how we react to our own flaws will determine how others react to them, too. If you're very brave, if you concentrate on how beautiful you are inside, then that's what your friends will see, too."

She sniffed and looked up at him hopefully. "Do you really think so?"

"I know so," he said, praying it would be so for her, praying that she'd chosen friends who wouldn't cruelly abandon her.

"My dad can't even stand to look at me."

"Oh, baby, I'm sure that's not true."

"It is. He was here when Doc Wilding took off the bandages. He walked out and he hasn't been back. That was hours ago."

Frank wanted to curse the man's insensitivity, even though he could understand what a shock it must have been to see his once-gorgeous, vivacious teenager so cruelly scarred.

"I think maybe he's just hurting inside because of what happened to you," he said finally. "He's probably feeling a whole lot of guilt that he didn't do something to prevent it from happening."

"But the fire wasn't his fault," she replied adamantly. "He wasn't even home when it happened. He was away on a business trip."

"That's exactly what I mean. He's probably telling himself if he'd been there, it wouldn't have happened."

"He always told Mom not to smoke in bed. He told her," she said, her voice thick with sobs. She stared helplessly into Frank's eyes, touching his soul. "Oh, God, why did she have to do it anyway? Why didn't she listen?" And then in a low, sad cry, "Why did she have to die? I tried to get to her, but I couldn't, I just couldn't."

Frank felt as though every breath was being squeezed out of him as Pam revealed what had happened at home the night she'd suffered these terrible, disfiguring burns. He'd never known, never realized what torment this poor child was dealing with. It made his own injuries seem insignificant. For the first time since the accident, he realized how truly fortunate he had been. Pam had the additional burden of grief and guilt weighing on her, when recovery alone would have been challenge enough.

He stayed with Pam for what seemed like hours, rocking her in his arms, wishing he had the words or the certainty to swear to her that things would be okay. Finally he noticed a man only slightly older than himself standing in the hallway, his face haggard, his eyes red-rimmed. He motioned to him.

"Pam, honey," he said gently. "You've got company."

Pam slowly faced the door. "Daddy." Her voice quivered with hope and fear. This time her father didn't flinch, didn't look away. He moved to the other side of the bed and sat on the edge. Pam eased away from Frank and held out her hand. Frank held his breath until finally the other man grasped Pam's hand and pressed his lips to the scarred flesh. "I'm sorry I ran out before, baby."

"Oh, Daddy," she whispered.

Frank left them together, praying harder than he ever had in his life that they would be okay, that together they could handle the grief and anger and pain ahead.

He was greatly subdued when Jenny finally arrived at his house just after six. He led her into the kitchen, pointed out where things were, then sat at the table to watch as she immediately set to work. Her motions were efficient, yet he found them subtly provocative. Her quiet calm was soothing. There was comfort in her presence tonight, a comfort almost more important than the fierce longing that usually tormented him the instant she was near.

When the dinner was bubbling on the stove, she poured them each a glass of iced tea and sat down across from him. The look she directed at him was inquisitive.

"You've been awfully quiet ever since I got here. What's going on?"

"I saw Pam today after I left you."

She nodded, her own expression suddenly tired. "I heard you'd been visiting her regularly. She had a pretty rough time of it today. She said your visit helped."

Still troubled by the teen's anguish, he asked, "Will it get any better for her?"

"Not anytime soon. She has a lot of plastic surgery ahead."

Frank sighed wearily. "That poor kid. She could probably use some counseling as well. I had no idea how much she's been struggling to cope with."

"She's already seen the psychologist a few times. She'll make it. She's a fighter. She'll get past the shock of the scars and be ready to move on to the next step."

"That's what I told her. I found myself quoting you."

She grinned. "I'm glad something I said made an impression."

"Everything you said made an impression. I didn't always want to hear it."

"That's pretty much par for the course with burn patients."

He shook his head as he envisioned contending with emotional crises like Pam's day in and day out. "Jenny, why do you do this? How can you take it day after day? I know we talked about this before, but I'm just beginning to realize the toll it must take."

"It's what I do, the same way you're an artist. Can you imagine being anything else?"

"I suppose not, though I have been other things from time to time to help pay the bills."

"You've held other jobs," she corrected. "But only one career really means anything, right? I think maybe what I went through with my own surgery makes me even better able to deal with the fears patients have. I truly understand how scared they are, how damaged they feel."

The reminder of her cancer surgery surprised him. It was the first time she'd mentioned it since the day she first told him about it. He wanted to keep her talking, sensing that there were more things she needed to say, but probably never had. "Who's been there for you when you needed a shoulder to cry on?"

She dumped a spoonful of sugar into her iced tea and stirred it for so long he thought she might not respond. Finally she said with studied nonchalance, "Family, friends. Otis was with me when I went into the operating room. Usually the orderly just wheels you into pre-op, but he stayed right by my side until they put me under. I'll always be grateful to him for that."

Frank didn't even try to hide his dismay. "Your parents weren't here?"

She shook her head. "Actually I didn't tell them until after it was over. There wasn't any point in worrying them. There wasn't a thing they could do until I knew what I was up against."

Frank regarded her incredulously. "They could have been here for you. That's what families do. They share the bad times and make them a little easier."

She gave him a faint smile. "That's what *your* family does."

There was just a hint of envy in her voice. Frank wanted to say right then and there that it could become her family, too. The thought slammed into his consciousness like a car going sixty. In an instant of absolute clarity, he knew that was what he wanted more than anything else. He wanted to marry Jenny Michaels and teach her all about love and laughter and family, as she had taught him about fighting back and recovering. Although his physical wounds were not yet healed, thanks to her his emotional wounds were very nearly a thing of the past. He knew that no matter whether he carved again or not, he would be just fine as long as she was with him to make his blood race and his spirits soar. He could cope with whatever the future brought.

He also knew that she would run if he suggested it, if he dared to hint at what he was thinking. He couldn't imagine why she was so terrified of him. He'd never before encountered a woman so skittish. Megan had found being with him and his family totally comfortable. And his one or two other reasonably serious involvements had been with women who'd been quick to accept the idea of a relationship.

Not that he was such a prize, he amended quickly. But most women found him uncomplicated and nonthreatening. He tended to say what was on his mind.

The directness and lack of pretense appealed to women who'd encountered too little of either. Jenny was clearly the exception. She regarded him every bit as warily as she might a snake . . . or a notorious Don Juan. Who had created this distrust in her? Was he the specific target or was it all men? He had to understand her before he could expect to make any progress.

Jenny had moved back to the counter to roll out the biscuit dough she'd prepared earlier.

"Any special man in your life?" he inquired lightly, reopening a topic she'd successfully evaded in the past.

The rolling pin hit the dough with a thud. "I thought we'd discussed this."

"We did. Your answer wasn't very illuminating."

"Why do you want to know?" she said as the pin hit the dough again, sending a puff of flour into the air like late-afternoon fog rising on San Francisco Bay. Her gaze was carefully averted. Biscuit dough had apparently never been so fascinating.

"Curiosity," he admitted candidly.

"Prying is more like it."

"Let's try this from a different direction," he said. "How do you spend your spare time? You can't possibly read medical journals every night."

"Actually I could, but I don't."

"When you're not reading them, what do you do?"

He caught the subtle hesitation before she said, "I go to movies."

"Good. Now we're getting somewhere. I like movies." He listed several. She hadn't seen any of them.
"What was the last movie you saw?"

She frowned, then finally named one.

"Sure," he said cheerfully. "I remember that one.
It won an Academy Award."

She blinked at him. "It did?"

"Sure did." He paused, then added, "Last year."

"Oh." Her voice was meek. Her fascination with
the biscuit dough increased. If she rolled it any flatter
there wasn't a baking powder in the world that could
make those biscuits rise higher than a silver dollar.

"So far we've accounted for one night in the last
year that you didn't read a medical journal. Anything
else?"

"Aerobics class," she said in a rush, looking ridic-
ulously pleased with herself. "I take aerobics."

"And?" he prodded.

"And what?"

"There has to be more, I mean for a woman with an
active social life such as yourself."

"We go out to dinner after class."

"We?"

"A friend and I."

"Must be a woman friend."

She glared at him. "Why must it be a woman? Men
take aerobics."

"But if it had been a man you'd have told me all
about him ten minutes ago to get me to shut up and
leave you alone."

Ignoring his comment, she cut out half a dozen very flat circles and slapped them onto a cookie sheet, then put the tray into the oven.

"They'll do better if you turn on the heat."

She whirled on him then, flour-covered hands on slim hips. "I don't have to do this, you know."

"I know," he said very seriously. "Why are you doing it? Why did you come?"

"Because you asked me to. You said you needed help."

"I need you," he corrected.

She was shaking her head in denial before the words were out of his mouth.

"It's true," he insisted. "In fact, I think if I don't kiss that smudge of flour on your nose within the next ten seconds I might very well die."

She stared at the floor until he reached out with the tip of his finger and tilted her chin up. Her gaze was defiant.

"Do it, then," she challenged. "Just do it and get it over with."

He grinned at her attempt to stare him down. "You're not going to shame me into backing off, by implying that I'm pushing you into something you don't want."

A reluctant sigh shuddered through her. "Who says I don't want it?" she asked.

Frank was taken aback by the hard-won admission. "Oh, Jenny," he murmured, drawing her slowly into his arms. With a sigh of his own, he settled his lips on hers. After an instant of stunned stillness, her arms circled his neck. Her body melted against his. Her skin was warm and flushed from bending over the stove. Her soft springtime scent drifted around them. She tasted of tea and sugar and a dusting of flour. It he held her in his arms like this for a lifetime, he knew his hunger for her would never be sated.

His fingers traced the line of her brow, the curve of her jaw. With each touch, she trembled. With each touch, his need built. One kiss would never be enough. He wanted to discover everything about her, every curve, every texture, every taste. His hand slid to her hips and tilted them up tighter until neither of them could deny the heat or the urgency. Then, without thinking of anything except the hunger to know every shape, every intimate detail of her body, he touched her breast, the caress as natural and needy as breathing.

With a startled cry, she broke free.

"No," she whispered tearfully, backing away. "No. This can't happen. Not ever."

And then she ran.

Nine

When the realization of what he had done slammed into him, Frank cursed himself for an insensitive fool. By the time he recovered from the shock of Jenny's anguished reaction to his touch, she had left the house, leaving the door wide open behind her. He raced outside and saw that in her haste to escape, she'd simply run, leaving her car parked halfway down the block. He took off down the hill after her.

He caught up with her at the corner. She was huddled under the street lamp, her arms hugging her middle against the chilly night air that plagued San Francisco even in May. She stood perfectly still, as if she couldn't make up her mind what to do next, where to go. With the silver mercury light filtering down on her through the fog, she looked lost and alone, so terribly alone. He reached out to her, but she seemed to withdraw to some safe and distant place he couldn't reach. As he put his hands in his pockets, Frank felt the painful wrench of her hurt deep inside.

"Jenny, please," he said urgently. "I'm sorry. I didn't mean to upset you. I wasn't thinking. I just knew how much I wanted you, how much I thought you wanted me. Let's talk about what happened, about why you're so scared. We can work this out."

"There's nothing to talk about," she said flatly. "Nothing."

The emptiness in her voice shook him, but the determination was worse. How could he fight that? "At least come back to the house," he urged as a first, crucial step. "It's too cold to be out here without a jacket."

As if to prove his point, she shivered. He pressed her then, afraid that she'd wind up sick if she stubbornly insisted on staying outside much longer. "I promise not to bring up what happened until you're ready," he said with reluctance. "And I won't touch you, if that's the way you want it."

Her eyes reflected her distrust and again he cursed himself. How much damage had he done in that one careless moment? In instinctively seeking to touch her breast, to discover every shape and texture of her, apparently he had reminded her graphically of her own fears of being an incomplete woman, her obviously deep-seated terror that she couldn't satisfy a man. Because she radiated such strength and self-confidence, he had forgotten that she was a special woman with a need for very special care, especially the first time they became intimate. He owed her all of the gentle tenderness that she had shown him when it came to his own scars.

Now he could only wait and pray that the damage of his gesture wasn't irreparable. Eventually a sigh seemed to shudder through her. Without a word, she began to slowly climb the hill. When she didn't stop at her car, Frank released the breath he'd been holding.

When they were finally outside his house, she stopped and looked up. The faint beginnings of a smile tugged at the sad, downturned corners of her mouth. "You did it," she said in a trembly voice. Tears she hadn't shed earlier sparkled in her eyes. "You painted it blue. I didn't notice when I came in."

"Jared finished yesterday. You chose the color, remember?"

She looked from the house to him and back again. "I was right," she said finally.

"About what?"

"It does match your eyes."

He chuckled. "So that's what Karyn's been gloating about. She guessed, didn't she?"

"She never said, but I think so."

"There's a touch of the romantic in you after all, isn't there, Jenny Michaels?"

She immediately shook her head in denial. "I'm a hard-headed realist. Ask anyone."

"You'd like to believe that, because it's safe, but it's not true," he said just as adamantly. "You have the same dreams as any other woman."

"What makes you think you know anything about a woman's private dreams, especially mine?" she said, a trace of anger in her voice, but an expression of undeniable yearning on her face.

"I know because you shared them with me in that kiss. We felt the same things, the same wanting not to be alone, the same need to love."

There was a spark of defiance in her eyes. "Chemistry. Pheromones. Lust. Not dreams."

"Oh, no," he said with certainty. "A woman like you could never separate the two. You would never let some casual lover get that close. You wouldn't take the risk of being rejected." He knew he was taking a risk himself by so bluntly stating the facts as he saw them.

For an instant, Jenny looked as though he'd slapped her. Then, to his relief, she began to laugh. "Giving me a taste of my own medicine, aren't you? No man's ever been that direct with me before."

He stared at her for several heartbeats, then said gently, "Maybe no man has ever cared as much as I do." He held out his hand. "Come inside."

It was ten seconds, thirty, an eternity before she sighed deeply and slid her hand into his.

Inside, Frank was careful to keep his distance, to let Jenny set the tone and the pace. The thawing of icy tension was slow, but eventually they laughed about the hard-as-rocks biscuits and savored the rich beef stew. They talked about old movies—the only ones

Jenny really had seen—and about sports. To his astonishment, she was both an avid football fan and an ardent baseball fan. Unfortunately she foolishly preferred the Boston teams to his own 49ers and Giants. She cited flimsy statistics in support of her imprudent loyalty.

"I hope you don't actually bet on your convictions with Otis," he teased, relieved that they were close to recapturing the earlier friendly tone.

"I don't bet anything with Otis," she reminded him. "Though goodness knows, he tried to convince me to wager against him by offering outrageous spreads. What the devil is a point spread anyway?"

"Considering your views on the evils of gambling, you don't want to know. You'd probably confiscate his paycheck and make him live on an allowance."

"I can just see him agreeing to that."

Frank laughed with her, then turned serious. "I doubt you have any idea just how persuasive you are. I think you could get a man to agree to just about anything."

She looked startled, then pleased. She held his gaze for just an instant before looking nervously away and getting to her feet. "Even helping with the dishes?" she said with the kind of rush born of deep-rooted caution. She was not going to make things easy for him. There would be no overnight burst of faith, no quick readjustment of her tendency to hide behind a brusque professionalism.

He wiggled his inept fingers at her. "I don't have enough dishes in the house for me to go tampering with the ones I do have."

"You could manage if you really wanted to," she countered, the mood settling comfortably at last into the light banter with which she obviously felt more at ease. "I seem to recall that you have a particular aversion to doing dishes. I think you're just using your injury as an excuse to get out of helping."

He grinned back at her. "But you'll never know for sure will you?"

"Maybe not," she said as one of his few good plates seemed to slide from her grasp. With his lightning-quick reflexes, Frank caught it in midair.

"Then, again," she observed, amusement dancing in her eyes, "looks to me like your recovery's a whole lot further along than you've been letting on."

"You little rat," he muttered. "You did that on purpose to test me."

She grinned. "You bet. You wash. I'll dry."

For the first time in his life, Frank actually enjoyed doing dishes. He was tempted to pull out every mismatched plate, every scarred mug and chipped cup in the cabinets just to keep Jenny around a little longer. He knew that the minute they were done, she'd go, fleeing her emotions, chasing the illusion of safety.

In fact, as it turned out, she had her jacket on and her car keys in her hands before he could drain the water from the sink. He didn't waste time arguing with her.

"I'll walk you to your car."

Wishing he could do the gallant thing and open the door for her, he stood by helplessly while she unlocked the car and got in. "Thanks for tonight," he said, when she'd rolled down the window.

Jenny nodded, her face upturned expectantly as if waiting for his kiss. Frank leaned down and brushed his lips across hers, fighting against the urge to linger and savor the velvet warmth. "It's not over, Jenny Michaels. Not by a long shot."

He whistled as he turned and walked back up the hill. It was a very long time before he heard the car start and saw Jenny drive off.

Frank made a resolution as he lay awake later that night. With the finely honed instincts of a man used to caring for others, he had seen through Jenny's veneer of steel to the fragility and insecurities underneath. For the first time he realized that the complexities of his own recovery were nothing compared to hers. She had taught him all about acceptance and fighting back. He was about to teach her all about joyous, unconditional love. Though his financial future was uncertain, he could offer her that much at least.

He would start his fight to overcome Jenny's shattered self-esteem with tender, potent kisses. He had seen the longing in her eyes, so much longing that it made him tremble. And, no matter what she said, there was no doubting that she had kissed him back. She would again. It would just take some old-fashioned wooing.

He might, he decided reluctantly, have to get a few tips on that from his experienced baby brother.

Tim was delighted to help out with some expert advice over lunch the next day. So, unfortunately, were Kevin, Jared, Peter and Daniel, who turned up en masse. The word that big brother had the hots for the therapist spread through the Chambers clan faster than a wildfire on a windy day. Even Karyn, still in Indianapolis with Brad for the Indy 500 trials, knew by dinnertime. She called just to stick in her two cents.

"I knew it," she gloated. "I knew that she was crazy about you the day she came out of your room all hot and bothered because you wouldn't do your therapy."

Frank groaned, tempted to hang up on her, but unwilling to give her the satisfaction. "Karyn, at that point the woman had spent approximately fifteen minutes with me and I was not especially charming. I don't think she was smitten. I think she was mad."

"Anger. Passion," she said dismissively. "They're both pretty powerful emotions. People get them confused all the time."

"Another five minutes of this and I am going to get passionately angry at you."

"Don't threaten me," she countered cheerfully. "It's payback time. You've been meddling in our lives from day one. Do you recall the night you stormed into Brad's hotel to rescue your precious baby sister from his evil clutches?"

"Only too well."

"I've never been so humiliated in my entire life. I may not rest until I've had a chance to get even."

"The man lied and said you weren't there," he reminded her. He was still none too pleased about that, but he had to admit that Brad was treating Karyn okay. The two of them were obviously crazy in love.

"He lied to protect my honor," she said. "It's about time you forgave him for that. Now let's talk about you. Forget anything Tim or the rest of those chauvinistic brothers of ours told you. Here's how you go about winning Jenny's heart. Trust me..."

Jenny did not sleep well, not that night, not for days. Like an old-fashioned newsreel, the scene in Frank's kitchen played through her head. Her panic was just as real in the middle of the night as it had been at the time.

Only once since the surgery had she allowed a man to touch her as intimately as Frank had. She had thought she loved Larry Amanti, thought he loved her. He had been warned about the scar. He'd told her it didn't matter, had sworn that he loved her just as she was. Then, when he had stripped away her clothes, when she was naked and vulnerable, she had seen the flicker of revulsion in his eyes, had shivered as he tried desperately to overcome his instinctive reaction and touch her anyway. Humiliated beyond belief, she had yanked the sheet around her and ordered him from her bed. He had fled, gratefully if the look in his eyes had been anything to go by.

In the days and months that followed, she'd realized that perhaps she was the one who had overreacted. With her insecurities close to the surface, she had never given him a chance to adjust to the disfigurement for which no amount of advance warning could adequately prepare a man. Even with that new self-awareness, though, she was not prepared to take the risk again. Rejection was always painful, but it would be doubly so if it came from a man like Frank, a man with whom she'd fallen hopelessly in love because of his kindness and sensitivity.

Although she couldn't bring herself to turn Frank's therapy over to Carolanne—it would be an open admission to him that she did fear what was happening between them—she did keep her distance. Not once over the next couple of weeks did she squeeze his shoulder in encouragement or place her hand on his to add pressure to his grip. The slightest contact seemed to stir desires she had no business having. It was better not to feel that flaring of heat, better not to respond to that tug deep within her, better not to experience the racing of her pulse.

To her chagrin, Frank seemed oblivious to the withdrawal of physical contact. If anything, he was even more businesslike than she was. He smiled. He joked. He even winked on occasion, a gleam of pure devilment in those wicked blue eyes of his. But his attention never wandered very far from the exercises. When the sessions were over, he thanked her politely and went off to visit with Pam, leaving Jenny vaguely discontented and out of sorts. He was doing exactly as she wanted, wasn't he? So why did she feel so damned lousy?

One day, feeling thoroughly abandoned, she followed him down the hall, then lingered outside Pam's room as the two laughed uproariously over stories she couldn't quite overhear. She hated to admit, even to herself, how much she missed that easy camaraderie, the teasing banter, the undeniable sexual overtones that made her pulse tremble.

"Eavesdropping?" Otis inquired from behind her.

Jenny backed up so fast she almost stumbled over his big feet. "No, of course not," she said.

Otis shook his head and rocked back on his heels. "You two got to be carrying on the strangest romance I ever did see."

Though her cheeks burned with embarrassment, Jenny retorted quickly and, she hoped, convincingly, "Romance? There's no romance between Frank and me."

Otis rolled his eyes. "You expect me to believe that? I've seen the way you've been mooning around here the last couple of months."

"Yes, I do expect you to believe it, because it's true."

"Oh, Jenny, Jenny. Are you just lying to me or to yourself, too?"

"Go away, Otis."

He grinned at her. "I'm going," he said. "By the way, I'm betting on a fall wedding. Don't let me down. I've got a bundle riding on it."

Horrified, Jenny chased after him. When she caught him, she backed him against the wall, fire in her eyes. "Who would you make a bet like that with?" she demanded. "Otis, if you've been spreading gossip all over this hospital, you are history, dead meat..." She searched for a fate so terrifying it would put the fear of God into him.

"Don't go getting yourself in a dither. The bet's with Pam."

"Pam?" she repeated incredulously. Her friend, her pal, was engaging in bets with Otis behind her back? And about her wedding to a man she was barely even speaking to?

"She's betting on May," Otis said cheerfully. "Personally, I don't think either you or Frank is smart enough to make a move that fast. Only a few more days left in the month. Told her that, too, but the kid's a real romantic. She really wants a May wedding. She's probably in there right now working on Frank."

Jenny clenched her teeth. "There will be no wedding," she said slowly and emphatically. "Not in May. Not in the fall. Not ever."

Otis's smile spread across his face. "You want to make a bet on that, too? I'll give you great odds. Wouldn't even mind losing this one. I like the man. I think he's good for you. Puts a little color in your cheeks. Like now. Pink as can be."

Jenny groaned and went back to the therapy room, where she threw every piece of foam rubber in the place as hard as she could. When that didn't even dent her frustration, she started on noisier supplies. The door opened just as a jar sailed across the room. Frank ducked as it shattered mere inches from his head.

"Having a bad day?" he inquired lightly.

"A bad day. A bad week. A bad month."

"Something happen after I left?"

"No." Nothing that she was about to admit to him.

"Been to that aerobics class lately?"

"What aerobics—" She stopped herself as she recalled that she'd told him about the way she spent her evenings. "Oh, of course, I told you about those. I forgot."

"Forgot you told me or forgot to go?"

She was very tempted to tell him to go to hell just to wipe that smug grin from his face. Instead she inquired testily, "Did you come back for a reason?"

"Sure did. I meant to tell you earlier that Tim got tickets for a Giants game tonight. He can't go. Want to come with me?"

Peanuts, popcorn and Cracker Jacks, all the lures of the song about the ballpark tempted her to say yes. "It wouldn't be a date or anything, right?"

He nodded agreeably. "Whatever you say."

How much trouble could she possibly get in with thousands of people around? Frank would be so busy yelling, he wouldn't even have time to notice her. Lately he hadn't seemed to notice her all that much anyway. "Okay," she said finally. "What time?"

"Now," he said at once.

"Now?"

"I didn't want to give you time to think it over and back out. Let's go."

During the first inning, Jenny was thoroughly self-conscious. She kept waiting for Frank's hand to squeeze hers, for his arm to slide around the back of her seat, for one of those bone-melting looks. His eyes never once left the ball field, and his hands were occupied with those peanuts and that popcorn she'd been daydreaming about earlier. She munched her own popcorn in oddly disgruntled silence.

By the third inning, she was just hoping for some small sign that he remembered she was there at all. When a soft-drink vendor passed by on the aisle, Frank actually blinked, glanced in her direction and inquired if she wanted anything. She was absurdly grateful for the attention and took a soft drink she didn't even want.

When the crowd stood for the seventh-inning stretch, Jenny decided there was no longer anything to fear . . . or hope for. Frank had brought her to a ballgame because he knew she liked baseball. It wasn't part of some grand seduction scheme. Why did that seem to irk her so when she had no intention of letting their relationship progress?

She was still pondering that when the game ended with a winning bases-loaded homer by the Giants center fielder. Suddenly Frank's arms were around her and he was swinging her in the air. His genuine exuberance was contagious. She was still laughing with him when the innocent embrace turned serious.

She slid slowly down the length of his body as he lowered her feet to the ground. She was aware of every inch of contact, every exciting flare of heat between them. Her breath left her as her toes touched down. Fortunately Frank showed no intention of releasing her. If he had, she was certain her knees would have buckled.

His gaze searched her face, his blue eyes darkening with desire. Her own heart was pounding.

"Oh, damn," she murmured finally as the strength for the battle with her own emotions ebbed.

Frank gave a low chuckle at her heartfelt sigh. "Yeah, I know what you mean."

"You did this deliberately, didn't you?"

"Did what?"

"Kept your distance until tonight, until just now?"

"I was advised by an expert that heightened anticipation can accomplish miracles."

Jenny felt something shift inside her at his hopeful expression. "Frank, don't," she warned, but without much force.

He grinned at her faint warning. "Don't waste your breath. This is one argument you will never win. I intend to prove to you that what we have isn't going to vanish overnight, that it isn't some quirk of the patient-therapist relationship. I love you, Jenny Michaels, and one of these days you're just going to have to accept that."

Jenny wanted to. Dear God, how she wanted to. But fate had dealt both of them a couple of low blows. She didn't trust it not to have another one in store.

Ten

It took Frank three weeks after the baseball game to convince Jenny to once again spend some time with him outside of the hospital. She displayed an inordinate amount of distrust of his motives. No doubt that had something to do with the undeniable arousal he was sure she'd detected when he'd taken her into his arms in the bleachers at the end of the game. It they'd been anywhere but in the middle of a stadium, she might not have escaped so easily. At the very least, he would have kissed her the way he wanted to, slowly and deeply and convincingly.

"Hey, I'm fighting for my life here," he teased, trying to overcome her reluctance with the humor she seemed to prefer to serious declarations. "What's one measly little afternoon? Surely you can trust yourself not to attack me and ravish me in that length of time.''

Her brows rose a disapproving fraction. "I'm not the problem," she reminded him pointedly.

"Handcuff me," he suggested.

She chuckled at the outrageous option. "I don't think we need to go that far."

Frank seized the faint hint of surrender. "You're wavering. I can tell. What'll it take? A promise written in blood? A chaperon? I'll even ask Karyn to fly home and take your side. She'd love the chance to give me a little grief. She claims I made her dating life a living hell."

Jenny immediately appeared fascinated. "How? Too protective?"

"Maybe a little," he admitted ruefully. "She's itching to even the score. I will invite her, though. Just say the word."

"No," she said finally. "I guess I can trust you."

"Your faith is overwhelming."

"Don't pout. Besides, I'm not finished. I'll agree to see you, but only if I get to choose what we do. Something therapeutic."

Frank groaned, but agreed. "Anything you say. What's it going to be?"

"You'll see," she said with an unexpectedly impish little gleam in her eyes. "Sunday afternoon at three. Be ready. I'll pick you up."

Frank was so enthralled by the gleam in her eyes, so caught up in the seductive possibilities, that he forgot all about the Chambers Sunday dinner tradition.

When his mother called that night to remind him, as she had every week since he'd moved out of the family home, he braved her wrath and announced, "Can't make it this time, Ma. I've got an important date."

Her startled silence lasted no more than a heartbeat. "Important?" she repeated with obvious fascination. "You'll bring her along. That's no problem."

"It's a problem. She's already made plans."

"What plans?"

"I don't know. It's a surprise."

"Well, you just surprise her and tell her you're coming here. Is it Jenny?"

"Yes."

"Wonderful. She'll fit right in. Four o'clock, same as always."

She hung up before he could argue. Maybe they could do both, he thought reluctantly. Maybe Jenny wouldn't mind at least dropping by for dinner, though the prospect of subjecting her to the fascinated examination of his family on a more concentrated level than the ones she'd been exposed to at their hospital visits was daunting. Tim and the others were not known for their subtlety. The already-skittish Jenny was likely to take off before dessert and never speak to him again.

He hadn't been off the phone five minutes when it rang again.

"Frank?"

From the sudden leap of his pulse, he would have known it was Jenny, even if he hadn't recognized that tentative note in her voice. The only time she ever sounded that uncertain was when she was talking to him about their relationship, rather than the progress of his therapy. "Hi. Didn't we just see each other? You aren't calling to cancel our date already, are you?"

"I'm not sure. I just had the oddest call from your mother."

Frank muttered a curse under his breath. He should have guessed she'd leave nothing to chance. "What did she want?" he inquired, though there wasn't a doubt in his mind that she'd taken that Sunday dinner invitation into her own capable hands.

"She said she wanted to personally invite me over on Sunday. She seemed to think you might not relay the message, something about a traditional family dinner."

"An astute woman, my mother."

"Frank, is your family getting the wrong impression about us?" Jenny definitely sounded troubled.

"I doubt it," he said. "It seems to me they've got it pegged."

"What?" She sounded even more alarmed.

"Never mind," he said quickly. "What did you tell Ma?"

"What could I say? I told her I'd be delighted, but Frank, I am not delighted." Each word was said with slow emphasis.

"Then we won't go. I told my mother we had plans."

He heard Jenny's deep sigh. "I tried that, too. She doesn't seem to take no for an answer. That's when I caved in and said yes. That woman should pick a charity and become a fund-raiser. She'd rake in millions."

"Believe me, I know the feeling. Trying to argue with her is like jogging straight into a brick wall. It's up to you, though. We do not have to go, no matter what you told her. I'll take care of it. I don't want you to feel uncomfortable," he said, though, now that he thought of it, the idea of watching Jenny interact as a part of his family held an undeniable appeal.

Now that she knew she had his support, she seemed to hesitate. "Is everyone going to be there?"

"Everyone. I think these Sunday dinners were part of the compromise when we all started to move out. We swore that we would always come back once a week."

"Then you can't very well back out of this one. You go. We'll do something another time."

Frank grabbed desperately at the first response that came to him. "And have my entire family know that you broke our date because you were scared of them?"

"I'm not scared of them," she countered. "Well, not exactly, anyway. I just don't want them to get the idea that there's anything serious between us."

"It might be too late for that," he admitted. "They all know how I feel. If you don't show up Sunday, I guarantee each one of them will probably pay you a visit to tell you what a great guy I am. I don't think any of them will beat you up..."

He allowed the possibility to linger before adding, "They're not usually violent. We all do tend to be pretty protective though."

There was a long pause before Jenny said, "Are you saying I might have to listen to six separate sales pitches on your behalf?"

"Seven. Ma's a real tigress. Come to think of it, *she* might beat you up."

Jenny finally started chuckling. "You're teasing me, aren't you?"

"Oh, no, sweetheart. This is gospel."

"It might almost be worth it to stay home and see who turns up to list your attributes."

"You already know my attributes. Well, most of them, anyway. I'd be glad to share the rest anytime you're ready."

"I'll just bet you would. Okay, forget my surprise. We'll go to dinner with your family. But I swear to you, if the words wedding or marriage even creep into the conversation in a whisper, I'll turn you over to Otis."

"That's no threat," he scoffed. "He's on my side."

"I was hoping you didn't know that."

"I'm sure you were. See you Sunday."

Frank found himself looking forward to the prospect with a very odd mixture of buoyant optimism and gut-deep dread. The combined forces of all the Chambers would either win Jenny over, or scare her away for good.

Jenny stood outside the Chambers's small, unpretentious home, Frank beside her, and battled the flutter of a thousand butterflies in her stomach. A fresh coat of paint in sedate white lost its innocent air in the red trim. The combination reminded her of the family, old-fashioned with an intriguing hint of quirky daring. Frank epitomized those qualities, though she doubted he saw himself that way.

There was no mistaking the fact that he'd been courting her for all these weeks now, setting a pace that was just shy and patient enough to relax her guard. At the edge of all that caution, though, was the sly promise of dangerous desires about to be unleashed. Jenny was captivated, despite her best intentions to maintain a careful distance between herself and the man who was so trustingly offering her his heart.

She'd been lured here today by curiosity and longing. It seemed like forever since she'd felt part of a family. Never had she even imagined belonging to a clan as boisterous and tight-knit as this one. She'd been unable to resist the chance to spend one brief afternoon in an environment filled with warmth and acceptance and love. It might be the only chance she ever had to experience what it could have been like had she dared to believe in Frank's love, had she dared to make a forever commitment. Though she would never have admitted it to him, she was indulging herself in a dream, a dream that was both alluring and forbidden.

"You're shaking," he observed, snapping her out of her lovely daydream. "Scared?"

"Of course not."

"Then you're a braver soul than I am," he said fervently, making her laugh and forget her fears.

"They're your family," she reminded him.

"Then my reaction ought to tell you something. Are you sure you wouldn't rather go skydiving?"

"Absolutely not. I can't wait to see why they have a grown man like you quaking in your boots."

He grinned and held out his hand. "Then let's get it over with."

Before they'd made it up the front walk, the door was thrown open. Mrs. Chambers, wearing a simple navy dress with a prim, lacy, white collar under her apron, waited for them with a beaming smile. She wiped both hands on the apron, then held them out to Jenny. "Welcome, Jenny. Come in. We've been waiting for you. Everyone's here."

As they walked toward the living room, Frank leaned down and whispered, "I warned you. They've never been on time before. Today they couldn't wait."

His mother hushed him. "Maybe they just knew I was making pot roast."

"Ma, you always make pot roast on Sunday."

"I do not. Just last week we had chicken."

"Tasted like pot roast to me," Frank said.

"Me, too," Tim concurred, popping into the hallway. "Looked like it, too. Must have been all those carrots and baby onions you used to hide the meat."

Mrs. Chambers glared indignantly at the pair of them. "Keep it up and there will be no apple cobbler for the two of you."

"Cobbler again?" Peter chimed in with an exaggerated groan as he joined them.

His mother waggled a finger in his direction. "Just for that, you can set the table. Now. Jenny, you go on in the living room and sit down. Daniel, Kevin and Jared are in there. Don't let them gang up on you. If they start giving you a rough time, you can come hide out with me in the kitchen."

Jenny laughed. "I think maybe that's my first choice anyway. Can I come now? I'd like to help."

Frank's eyes widened in dismay. "Bad idea," he warned. "The woman will try to pry information out of you. No secret will be safe. She's going to want to know what your intentions are."

Mrs. Chambers patted Jenny on the shoulder. "Don't listen to a word he says. You come right along. The rest of you, play nice," she added in an echo of Jenny's own advice to Tim and Frank weeks earlier. Jenny understood now why Tim had teased her so over the comment.

Jenny had thought she'd feel safe in the kitchen, out of the reach of all those prying eyes, away from Frank's hopes and everyone else's expectations. And at first she did feel safe. At first it was comforting to be surrounded by the heavenly smell of the roast, the cinnamon-scented cobbler, the yeasty aroma of rising rolls.

"What can I do?" she offered.

"You can sit right over there and talk to me," Mrs. Chambers said, waving Jenny toward a curved breakfast area. She gave Peter a handful of silverware and shooed him toward the dining room. She brought over a bag of beans and began snapping them as she sat across from Jenny. "You've been seeing Frank for a while now, isn't that right?"

"At the hospital," Jenny replied cautiously, trying to decide if the question was innocuous or the start of an inquisition. She grabbed a handful of beans herself and clumsily tried to imitate Mrs. Chambers's quick, decisive motions.

Mrs. Chambers shot her a perceptive look. "Just another patient, right?"

"No, of course not. I mean . . . oh, dear," she murmured, falling neatly into the maternal trap set by Mrs. Chambers.

"Frank's a fine man," his mother reported.

"I know that."

"Took on a lot of responsibility at an early age."

"I know."

"Just look at this kitchen. He fixed it up for me, put in new cabinets, that fancy tile."

"It's beautiful," Jenny said honestly. The white, glass-fronted cabinets gave the room an open, airy feeling. The white tile floor and single row of red accent tiles amid the white on the walls added to the cheerful ambience. The built-in breakfast nook was a similar combination of white Formica and red seat covers. "Did Frank build this breakfast area, too?"

Mrs. Chambers beamed with pride. "Isn't it something? Used to be a pantry here. He knocked out the wall and the next thing you know the kitchen was nearly twice as big as it used to be. How many men would have thought to do that?"

Jenny admired all the extra touches that she was certain were Mrs. Chambers's, the framed prints on the walls, the bright dish towels, but Frank's mother wasn't interested in her own contribution. She was pushing her son's. In case Jenny hadn't gotten the message, she added, "He'd make a wonderful husband."

"Mrs. Chambers, really, Frank and I are just friends."

"Good way to start."

"Start?" Jenny said weakly.

"Of course. My husband and I started out as friends, too. Makes a lot more sense than the way kids do things these days. They fall into bed, get married and then discover they don't have a thing in common. Do things slow and you do them right. You two take your time, if that's what you need."

Suddenly the large room seemed to be closing in on Jenny. "But..." The protest was barely begun before it was interrupted.

"Of course," Mrs. Chambers said cheerily, "I always did think a fall wedding was mighty nice. The church could be decorated with bright yellow mums. Karyn would look real good in that coppery shade that you see in all the fancy fashion magazines."

"Karyn?"

"Of course, I don't mean to be pushy. I know you have your own friends, but I always think it's nice if someone from the groom's family stands up with the bride, too, don't you?"

"In theory," Jenny said, wondering desperately if there was any polite way she could escape to the living room or find a pit of vipers to throw herself into. If she stayed here much longer, she was liable to end up married before anyone heard her protests. She crumbled the beans in her hands into little, bitty pieces before she realized what she was doing.

The kitchen door swung open. "How's it going in here?" Frank inquired. "You two getting acquainted?"

"Oh, my, yes," his mother replied. "We were just discussing the wedding."

Frank's startled gaze shot to Jenny. His eyebrows rose a quizzical half inch. "Wedding?" he repeated. "Whose?"

"Why yours, of course," Mrs. Chambers said, back at the stove and still oblivious to Jenny's panic.

"Ma!"

She turned and waved a spoon at him. "It never hurts to give a girl a nudge, let her know she'll be welcome in the family."

A twinkle of amusement appeared in Frank's eyes as he scanned Jenny's face. She was sure she must be pale as a ghost. "You feeling welcome?" he asked.

"Very," she said, injecting the single word with ominous implications.

"Maybe you'd like to come back in the living room with me," Frank suggested hurriedly.

"I'd love to."

Mrs. Chambers gave them an approving smile. "You two go right along. I'm sure Jenny and I will have a chance to talk more later."

Jenny nearly moaned as she left the kitchen.

"I tried to warn you," Frank said, his arm circling her shoulder.

She twisted away from the embrace. "You're enjoying this, aren't you? You're letting your mother do your dirty work."

"What dirty work is that?"

"The woman practically proposed on your behalf."

His expression brightened. "Really? What did you say?"

"Say? She didn't want an answer. She took the answer for granted." Jenny knew her voice was climbing, knew that her attempts to cover her earlier irritation with humor were starting to fail her now. This was exactly what she had feared would happen. The whole Chambers family was going to sit around all through dinner staring at her, waiting for an announcement that was not going to come. And she was going to have to put up with it.

Why? she thought suddenly. Why shouldn't she just lay things on the line? Frank might be a little embarrassed at first, but wasn't that better than allowing this whole misunderstanding to get entirely out of hand? Or was the real problem that a tiny part of her wanted the charade to be perpetuated? If she were to be perfectly honest, hadn't she enjoyed sitting in that kitchen and playing prospective daughter-in-law?

Okay, yes, dammit! Was that so terrible? It wasn't going to happen, but couldn't she indulge herself for a few minutes or even a few hours in the fantasy of becoming Mrs. Frank Chambers?

She looked up at Frank then and caught the speculative spark in his eyes. It was as if he could read her mind, as if he knew that she was waging an internal war and laying odds on the outcome.

Before she could come to a final decision on whether to go or stay, the choice was taken out of her hands. Mrs. Chambers started putting food on the table and the next thing Jenny knew, she was seated beside Frank's mother and they were all holding hands to say grace. When Mrs. Chambers gave thanks that her oldest son had found such a pretty, kind woman, Frank squeezed Jenny's hand reassuringly. She caught herself blinking back the surprising sting of salty tears and trying desperately to hold back the flood of hope.

As they drove home, Frank marveled at the transformation that had come over Jenny during the afternoon and evening. From a shy, unwilling date, she had slowly fallen into the role of fiancée. Though he'd been ready to strangle his mother when he'd first walked into that kitchen, he had to admit now that he should be grateful. After a few token protests, Jenny had apparently taken to the idea. By the time they'd left she'd been teasing his brothers, beating them all at Monopoly and agreeing to return the following Sunday. He still wasn't sure exactly what had come over her, but he'd be damned if he'd complain about it.

"Did you have a good time?" he inquired as she sat beside him, her eyes closed, a pleased smile tilting the corners of her mouth.

"The best," she murmured.

"Did it have anything to do with me?"

She blinked and stared at him sleepily. "Of course, why?"

"Because a few hours ago, you were adamant about defining the parameters of our relationship in very businesslike terms. By the time we left my mother's, if I'm not mistaken, at least seven people were of the opinion that we're engaged. I'm one of them."

She sighed. "I never really said that, did I?"

"No, but you knew that was the impression and you didn't correct it. Why?"

Her lower lip was caught between her teeth as she obviously struggled with an answer. "I guess I just got caught up in a fantasy," she said slowly. "I'm sorry."

His heart thudding, Frank said, "It doesn't have to be just a fantasy. I love you, Jenny. You know that. I want to marry you." He pulled the car to the side of the road and touched her cheek, which was damp with unexpected tears. "I do love you, sweetheart."

Her fingers traced his jaw, then his lips as his breath lodged in his throat. "Oh, Frank, if only..."

"There are no 'if onlys,'" he said angrily. "All you have to do is say yes. One little word. Why is it so hard for you?"

"You know why," she said, her voice thick with tears.

"Then come with me, come home with me and let me show you that there is nothing, *nothing,* standing in our way."

Jenny's eyes were shining, her lips trembling, when she finally whispered, "Yes. I'll come with you."

He caressed her cheek, his thumb moving over the lush curve of her lower lip as his heart slammed into his ribs. Anticipation rushed through him, hot and sweet and urgent. Along with it came a faint anxiety that he was certain mirrored hers.

"You won't be sorry," he vowed to reassure them both. "You will never be sorry."

Eleven

Regrets and doubts rioted deep inside Jenny the instant she agreed to go home with Frank. But the temptation had proved too strong, the illusion too powerful. Caught up in it, she'd been unable to say no. She would give anything for this one night to be perfect. She didn't doubt, not for a second, that Frank would try to make it so. She didn't doubt that he loved her. Every considerate action spoke of the depth of his feelings.

But was love the only thing that mattered? She had doubts enough about that for the both of them.

Even so, there could be no backing out now, no second thoughts leading to a tearful withdrawal. When she had said yes, she had made a commitment, to him and to herself. It might last no longer than this one night, but it was a commitment just the same. And, like Frank, she believed in honoring her vows.

Inside his house, she caught him studying her, his expression thoughtful, worried. "Nervous?" he said.

Jenny nodded.

"Me, too."

It had never occurred to her that he might be every bit as scared as she was. His nervousness and his admission of it both charmed and reassured her.

"You can change your mind anytime," he said, his blue eyes serious. *"Anytime."*

Feeling stronger with each reassurance, she shook her head. "I won't change my mind," she said with absolute conviction. "I want to be with you more than I've ever wanted anything in my life."

He nodded and held out his hand. When she placed her hand in his, he rubbed the pad of his thumb across her knuckles, then lifted her hand to his lips, his gaze fastened on hers. Inside, she trembled with the magic of that tender gesture.

"Would you like a drink?" he offered. "I think I have some wine."

"Yes. Wine would be good," she said, though she wanted time more than she wanted the drink. She needed to accustom herself to being here, to the prospect of an almost-forgotten kind of intimacy. She needed to steel herself to the possibility of rejection. Though her heart told her that Frank would never ever hurt her intentionally, she knew that the faintest hint of revulsion in his eyes, the least sign of disappointment would be devastating. She had to prepare herself for that, had to be ready not to cast blame for something over which he might have no control.

As she waited for the wine, she walked down the hall to his workroom and flipped on the light. She breathed in the clean scent of the various woods, rubbed her fingers over the textures of his finished carvings. When she came to the unfinished blue jay, she recalled how she had guided his inept fingers in this very room, how she had badgered him until he began fighting back against his injury, fighting to regain his skill. Unless she was mistaken, there were fresh details on the piece, less delicate perhaps, but evidence that he was trying.

She sensed that Frank was standing in the doorway. Glancing over her shoulder, she smiled at him. "I hope you don't mind that I'm in here," she said, suddenly realizing that he might consider this an invasion of his privacy, a claim to intimacy that she didn't rightfully have.

"Of course not," he said, though his uneasiness contradicted the words. He came closer and handed her the wine.

"You've been working." She gestured toward the blue jay.

He shrugged, his expression unexpectedly vulnerable. "I'm trying."

"It's very good."

He shook his head and regarded the carving critically. "Not yet," he said, but there was a trace of hope even in the denial.

"I'm proud of you."

"I'm proud of you, too."

Startled, she stared at him. "Why?"

"For daring to take this step, for trusting me."

"It was time," she said simply, and knew it was true. She might have put off the action for a week or a month or a year, but emotionally she was as ready now as she was ever likely to be. No man was ever likely to be more right for her than this kind, gentle man who waited patiently for her to set the pace. She put down the glass he'd given her. "Frank, would you hold me?"

A slow smile trembled on his lips as he put aside his own glass. "I thought you'd never ask," he murmured, opening his arms then folding them around her.

Jenny rested her head against his chest, listening to the quickened beat of his heart and breathing in the faintly woodsy masculine scent of him. There was such comfort in his embrace, such a sense of coming home at last. And yet...

And yet there was the lightning-quick racing of her pulse. Warmth that had nothing to do with the comfort and everything to do with rising passion stole over her. When his lips finally, inevitably settled on hers, the lightning added thunder, the warmth became white-hot urgency. There was no rush to the kiss, no hurry to the slow exploration by his tongue, but deep inside her, need built feverishly, demanding more, demanding a more passionate pace. She appreciated the care he was taking, the gentle advances, but she hungered for desperate loving, loving that would carry her beyond thought to pure sensation, passion able to overshadow doubts.

Her fingers tangled in the dark midnight of his hair as she pressed him closer. Her now-sensitive lips brushed across stubbled cheeks, seeking, again, the velvet fire of his mouth. When one arm braced her back and the other tucked beneath her knees, she gasped in startled astonishment, then settled against his chest as he carried her down the hall and into his bedroom.

For a few seconds she registered the room's details, the clean, masculine lines, the cheerful colors, the clutter of framed family pictures crowded on the dresser, the haphazard toss of clothes scattered about by a man always in a rush... until now. Then Frank captured all of her attention, his eyes smoky blue with desire, his expression still anxious.

"You're sure," he said one last time.

Though her heart raced with something very much like sheer panic, Jenny nodded. "I'm sure," she whispered. Then, more loudly, "Very sure."

He stepped closer, his gaze locked with hers. With fingers that trembled, he traced the neckline of her blouse, leaving a trail of goose bumps along her neck. Scared as she had never been scared before, filled with a yearning deeper than any she had ever known, Jenny allowed him to slowly, carefully, unbutton her blouse. With the release of the first button, she stilled, but the press of his lips against the newly exposed flesh had her quivering with need. His touch was so deft, his kisses so potent that she forgot to watch for the revulsion in his eyes as first her blouse, and then her specially designed bra fell away. All she remembered were the nights she'd lain awake imagining being cherished like this.

When she first felt his lips against the scar, a cry of dismay gathered in her throat, but before she could utter a single sound, she was lost in the sensations he aroused, the fierce tug deep in her belly, the sweet, aching hunger below. She wanted nothing more than to go on feeling, but she had to know. She had to.

At last she opened her eyes. With a mixture of awe and dread, she observed him as he gently traced the line of the scar. With her breath caught in her throat, she waited for him to back away, but the only sign of emotion was the tear that tracked down his cheek and the faint trembling of his hand as he touched her. He lifted his head, though his hand continued to stroke and caress and inflame.

"I love you, Jenny Michaels," he said, his gaze locked on hers.

"I love you," he whispered again, as his gaze slid lower to the scar and lingered there. There was an instant when he seemed to freeze, and Jenny felt her heart go still. Then she realized that he was staring at his own fresh scars, seeing the cruelly reddened skin against the whiteness of her flesh. She captured his hand in hers and kissed each finger until he, too, believed in the healing power of love.

Her own tears falling, mingling with his, Jenny heard the tender endearments, felt the powerful stirring of her body responding to his touch. Eyes closed, she gave herself over to the feelings, savoring them as a treasure she would hold always. Even after he'd gone.

That these wonderful, wild sensations couldn't last seemed a certainty. She wouldn't dare to hope beyond tonight, beyond this sweet, thrilling moment. With the fascination of a woman capturing dreams enough for a lifetime, she studied the magnificent lines of his body, the sculpted flesh with its richness of texture. No wonder that he created perfection with his carving knife, when he'd been given such an example. She traced each hardened muscle, each curve and indentation until she knew him as well as she knew herself, until his body tensed with need.

When their touches grew more frenzied, when their blood flowed like warm honey, when their thoughts had given way to pure sensation, they came together at last. Years of pain and hurt and doubting vanished in one shuddering moment of exultation. Love, as fresh and new as springtime, flowered in Jenny's heart.

As she curved her body against his, she told herself that forever was within reach. With his hands curved gently over her disfigured flesh, she could believe that she was beautiful and that anything was possible.

Awakening to find Jenny still in his arms filled Frank with a joy so profound it was as if he'd been reborn. He stretched cautiously, trying not to disturb her, then settled back to study the perfect silk of her skin, the tumble of curls with highlights the color of amber caught in the muted rays of morning sun. She was even tinier than he'd realized. His hands could probably span her waist. He rested one hand just above the curve of her hip to prove his point.

Beneath his touch, her flesh warmed and she began to stir. As she rolled onto her back, his fingers moved from hip to belly in a slow, sensual caress that changed the pattern of her breathing from restful to hurried. Hesitant to touch her breast, fearful that she would perceive the touch as a need she couldn't amply fulfill, he stroked the scar instead. Jenny whimpered, then sighed, then came slowly awake.

Frank smiled down at her, her sleepy sensuality an incredible turn-on that had him instantly hard and wanting. For an instant she remained open to him, then as if realizing her vulnerability, the exposure in daylight that hadn't existed the night before, she grabbed for the sheet. He reached out to stay her hands.

"Don't," he whispered, trying to quiet the panic in her eyes. Meeting that fearful gaze straight on, he said, "You are beautiful, a beautiful, desirable woman. Inside and out. And I could not possibly love you any more than I do right now."

Her lower lip quivered, and he wanted desperately to cover that faint trembling with his own lips, but he held back, knowing that the best proof was in not looking away. She would only believe him if he acknowledged the defect and showed her time and again that it didn't matter. It would take words and actions and time.

"You must believe me, Jenny," he said. "You are all the woman I need, and I will spend the rest of my life proving it to you."

Tears gathered in her eyes, then spilled down her face. She captured his scarred hand in hers and held it to her damp cheek. "I know that," she said with a sigh.

There was a hesitation in her voice, a shadow of doubt. "But you don't entirely trust what we have, do you? Why not? How can a woman who spends her life teaching others to look beyond scars, not see beyond her own?"

She drew away from him then, both physically and emotionally. He could read the distance in her sudden stiffness, the dullness that took the lively sparks from her eyes.

"Frank, it's not just the scars. If it was, don't you think I would throw myself into your arms and never let go? Last night was the most perfect night of my life. I felt fulfilled and complete and desirable. You did that for me. But I won't be one of those people you gather in and protect. You've already raised five brothers and a sister. You deserve a life that is carefree and filled with happiness."

Frank struggled to follow what she was saying. It made no sense. How could she equate herself with his family? It sounded as if she viewed herself as a burden, rather than an incredible woman to be treasured.

It sounded as if she planned to end things just as they were beginning.

"Jenny, this is crazy. I love you. I certainly don't think of you as some stray I have to take in and care for."

"But that could happen and I won't have it."

"Won't have what?" In his frustration, his voice rose to an irritated shout. "Dammit, talk to me. Make me see why you're willing to throw away what we have."

She turned pale at the thunder of his voice, but her voice was steady and bleak. "Because I don't trust it to last."

If she'd used the excuse that the sky might fall in a million years, he would have been no more confused. "Sweetheart, I know there are no guarantees, but why give up what we have now because of something that might never happen?"

"I don't like the odds."

"Odds? What odds? The fifty-percent divorce rate? What?"

"Stop yelling."

"I'm sorry. It's just that you're making me crazy," he said impatiently.

Her look quelled him. He took a deep breath. "Okay, talk to me. Make me understand. Are you worried about the way we met? Are you afraid that I've just grown dependent on you?"

Her expression softened. "No," she said, taking his hand and pressing a kiss to the knuckles. "You're strong now, and I know exactly what your feelings for me are. And I won't take advantage of that.''

"Take advantage how?"

She did grab the sheet then and tug it around her. When it was snug, when there was nothing for him to see below her bare shoulders, she said quietly, "What scares me more than anything is the possibility that I might become dependent on you."

"Jenny..."

She touched a silencing finger to his lips. "No, listen to me. It's been just about four years since the surgery. Five years seems to be the magic number in cancer survival. I'm still a long way from that. Every day I live with the reality that the cancer could come back. I won't burden you with that, I won't ask you to live each day with the possibility of a death sentence hanging over us." Her gaze met his. "I won't," she said with finality.

Frank struggled with the horrible possibility of losing her to a disease he thought she had conquered. His heart ached for her as he tried to imagine living with that fear of recurrence. And, yet, weren't they losing even more by living now as if the merely possible were certain? He had to make her see that.

Gently he brushed the tendrils of hair back from her face. He searched his heart for words that would be convincing. "Jenny, my love, haven't you ever listened to the wedding ceremony? In sickness and in health, remember that? You're healthy now. We have this moment in our lives. We'll take each tomorrow as it comes. If we don't, Jenny, if we turn our backs on this, what sort of memories will we have? Loneliness? Fear? Longing? I don't want that for myself. I don't want it for you. Maybe we'll never quite stop being afraid, but we certainly don't have to be alone.''

''It's not fair to you,'' she said stubbornly.

''It wasn't fair for you to get this disease. It wasn't fair for me to get burned. We both have to go on. It was your cancer and my burns that brought us together. Maybe we should concentrate on that and count our blessings.''

''I'm scared, Frank.''

''Of dying?''

''Of leaving you.''

''Then don't do it now, not while you have a choice in the matter.''

It was the most eloquent Frank had ever been, and he waited to see the effect of his words. For a moment as Jenny's arms slid around his waist, he thought he'd won. But then she rose, found the clothes they had tossed aside last night in their haste and, after sorting through them for hers, took them into the bathroom.

Frank wanted to throw something. He wanted to grab her by the shoulders and shout until she not only listened, but heard him. Instead he could only sit by helplessly as she did what she thought was right, what she thought was the noble thing.

When she came out of the bathroom, he held out his

hand. "Jenny, don't go. I'll fix breakfast. We'll talk this out."

Swallowing hard, she shook her head. Then she kissed him one last time, with tears in her eyes, and left.

Twelve

Letting Jenny go, admitting that he didn't know how to help her grapple with her fears that obviously tormented her, was the most difficult thing Frank had ever done. He'd wanted to fold her in his arms, to hold her and love her until she couldn't walk away, but something told him that would only make the leaving harder, not impossible. He, better than anyone, knew just how stubborn and determined she could be. Yet knowing that he'd done the right thing didn't make the days any easier.

Boredom, worse than anything he'd faced in the hospital, set in and, combined with the loneliness, made him cranky. By the end of the week, he was snapping at anyone who dared to set foot near him.

He tried carving again, but one slip of the knife had marred the blue jay he'd been struggling to complete and he'd tossed wood and knives into the trash. A day later he dug them out and tried again.

When Sunday rolled around, he begged off from the family dinner. He felt as though a lifetime had passed since the previous week, and he wasn't up to the questions and teasing innuendoes about a relationship that no longer existed. As soon as the excuses were out of his mouth, though, he knew it had been a mistake. By four, instead of gathering at his mother's, the whole clan began descending on him. Tim and Jared were the first to arrive.

"You look okay to me," Jared said after a close inspection.

"I'm fine."

"You told Ma you were sick," Tim reminded him.

"I think I'm coming down with something," he amended hurriedly. "I'm sure it's not serious, but it could be catching. You two go over to Ma's."

"We can't," Jared said.

"Why not? She'll be expecting you."

"No, she won't," Tim said, just as the doorbell rang. "That should be her now." He glanced at Jared. "I'm betting on chicken soup. How about you?"

"Broth. Beef broth and custard."

Frank groaned. "This is ridiculous. I am not that sick."

"Then you shouldn't have told her you were. Now we're all going to have to eat wimp food," Tim complained grumpily. "Do you have any idea how much I detest custard?"

There was a deeply offended gasp from the doorway. "What do you mean, Timothy Chambers? You've always said you loved my custard."

"Cripes, Ma, you weren't supposed to hear that."

"Then you shouldn't have said it, should you?" she said, hiding a grin. "Go out to the car and get the rest of the dinner."

"Real food?" Jared inquired hopefully.

"Soup and custard are real food. Now, go." Once they'd gone, she observed Frank closely and, with her finely tuned maternal radar, zeroed in on the real crux of his problem. "You and Jenny have a fight?"

"Why on earth would you ask that?"

"Otherwise, she'd be here nursing you."

"Ma, I think you've gotten the wrong idea about Jenny and me."

She shook her head. "I don't think so. What was the fight about?"

"It wasn't a fight exactly."

"What was it then *exactly?*"

"It's private."

She nodded slowly. "Okay. You do what you think is best, but, Son, don't turn your back on your feelings just because things aren't so smooth. If you love her, then you owe it to both of you to fight. Don't let it slip away because of false pride."

Frank didn't think pride had anything to do with letting Jenny leave, letting her make her own choices, but maybe it did. Maybe it had hurt, thinking that she didn't love him enough to try to save what they had. On the chance that his mother might be right, he made up his mind to go by the hospital on Monday, to talk to her and pester her until she saw that they could face the future and whatever it held—good or bad—a thousand times better together than they possibly could apart.

Energized by a stubborn determination of his own, and filled with hope, he strode through the hospital the next day, poked his head into Pam's room to say hello, then marched on to the therapy room like Sherman taking on Georgia. He pushed open the door and stepped inside, glancing first at Jenny's desk, then around the room. It was empty. The desk was ominously neat. He was still standing there trying to decide what to make of it, when Carolanne returned. She looked puzzled at finding him there.

"You here for a treatment?" she asked. "I don't recall seeing your name on the list for today."

"No. I'm here to see Jenny."

Her friendly expression closed down. "She's not in," she said, her tone cautiously neutral.

"I see that. Where is she?"

"She took a few days off."

Frank's heart began to thud dully in his chest. "Why? Is she okay?"

Carolanne studied him with serious gray eyes. "Come on in and sit down," she said finally. "I think it's time we had a talk."

Frank's pulse began to race. "Dammit, tell me where she is. What's happened?"

With the same spunkiness he'd encountered in
Jenny, Carolanne pointed toward a chair. "Sit. You
want some coffee?"

"Fine. Whatever," he said impatiently, but he sat.

A lifetime seemed to pass before she handed him a
cup of coffee, then pulled up a chair and sat opposite
him. "Are you in love with her?" she asked bluntly.

"Yes."

"Does she know it?"

"Yes," he said, oddly disquieted by the personal
questions, yet sensing that Carolanne really needed to
know if she was to be equally honest with him. "I've
told her."

She nodded thoughtfully. "That makes sense then."

"What makes sense? Dammit, would you stop
hedging and spit it out? Is she okay?"

"I don't know."

Frank felt as though the air were being squeezed out
of his chest. Before he could say a word, Carolanne
looked contrite and held up her hand apologetically.
"Sorry. I didn't mean to alarm you. I just mean that
she's undergoing some tests. Bone scans, liver scans,
blood tests, the works. It's routine in cases like hers,
but that doesn't mean it doesn't scare the dickens out
of her, out of all of us who love her. I don't know if
you can imagine what it's like waiting out the results,
waiting to find out if your life is hanging in the balance, if you're okay or doomed to undergo more surgery, more radiation, more chemotherapy, more hell."

Suddenly Frank made the connection between these
annual tests and Jenny's departure from his house.

"Did she know these tests were scheduled a week ago?"

Carolanne nodded. "I think she scheduled them three or four weeks back."

"Is she here in the hospital?"

"No, these are outpatient tests."

"Who's with her?"

"I'm not sure. I think Otis probably took the day off to drive her. He usually does, despite her arguments that she can do just fine on her own."

"What's her doctor's name?"

The therapist balked at that. "If she didn't tell you about the tests herself, then she won't want you turning up there."

"Don't you see? I have to be with her."

Carolanne continued to hesitate, then finally seemed to reach a decision. "Go to her apartment. She doesn't need you with her for the tests, but she will need you after. It's the waiting that's agonizing. She needs all the support she can get then." She dug in her purse and handed him a key. "Thank goodness I still have this from the first time I watered her plants, while she was back East. You know the address, right?"

"Yes. Thanks, Carolanne. I owe you."

"No. If you can make Jenny happy, that's all that matters. No one deserves a little happiness more than she does."

"I'm going to try like hell."

"You'd better. Otherwise, she'll kill me for giving out her key."

His first stop wasn't a florist, though that had been his first instinct. He'd dismissed the idea of filling the apartment with flowers as both too ordinary and too funereal. Frank opted instead for balloons, dozens of them in every color imaginable. Filled with helium, they floated in Jenny's living room like a rainbow sky. He ordered dinner from the finest restaurant in San Francisco and wine from the best Napa Valley vineyard. And, after determining that the test results would take days, he called a travel agent and ordered tickets for Hawaii to be delivered immediately by messenger. The impulsive, expensive vacation would dent his savings, but he couldn't imagine any gesture that would be a better use of his money. This was no time for caution. A little extravagance was called for.

With the tickets ordered, he sat back to wait, fully aware that his nervous anticipation was nothing compared to the dread that was likely to occupy Jenny's mind unless he could distract her. It was nearly five o'clock when he finally heard her key turning in the lock.

As the door swung open, setting a wave of balloons bobbing, an expression of delighted surprise spread across her face, wiping away the most obvious signs of weariness.

"Welcome home," he said softly, hiding his dismay at the shadows under her eyes, the slump of her shoulders that she couldn't hide.

"You did all this?"

Otis stood behind her, nodding in satisfaction. He gave Frank an approving thumbs-up gesture, then said, "Guess I'm not needed around here anymore. I'll just be on my way." When Jenny didn't even turn to look at him, his grin widened. "Tell her I said goodbye," he told Frank, feigning irritation. "If she happens to notice I'm gone."

"Bye," she murmured distractedly, apparently having caught just enough of Otis's words to realize he was leaving. Her gaze was riveted on Frank. "Why?"

"Because it's time you and I came to an understanding," he said matter-of-factly.

She stared at him in obvious confusion. "About what?"

"About the way things are going to be from now on. You were there for me when I needed help, when I was facing the toughest days of my life. From now on I'm going to be here for you. That's just the way it is. Like sunrise and birds singing and tides changing. Don't fight it, Jenny. I can't let you win this one."

There was a spark of fire in her eyes, then a flicker of acceptance. She sighed heavily and sank onto the sofa. Her whole body seemed to slump with exhaustion. "I'm so tired. I don't think I could battle a feather and come out on top right now."

Sensing victory, though not especially happy about the cause of her token protest, Frank pressed. "Does that mean you accept this as a done deal? You and me? Together, always?"

"We'll see," she said weakly, her eyes drifting shut as she curled into a more comfortable position.

It wasn't the commitment he'd hoped for, but at least she wasn't fighting him. Worried by her lack of energy, by her pale complexion, Frank settled beside her and pulled her into his arms. With a quiet sigh, she rested against him. "Oh, Jenny," he whispered as he listened to the even rise and fall of her breath. "Don't you dare leave me."

She murmured something in her sleep, then was quiet. Holding her in his arms filled Frank with the greatest contentment he'd ever known, even as his heart ached with the uncertainty of the future.

Jenny only dimly remembered coming home from the day of medical tests. Nerves, rather than the tests themselves, always took everything out of her. By the time she got home she felt limp as a dishrag. She remembered coming in. She remembered collapsing onto the sofa. She remembered . . . A puzzled frown knit her brow. Had Frank been there? Had he issued some sort of crazy ultimatum or had that been a lovely dream? She drew in a deep breath and slowly opened her eyes. Then she blinked and blinked again. One part of the dream at least had been real.

Jenny had never seen so many balloons before in her life. Laughter bubbled up as she stared at the reds and greens, blues and yellows bobbing above her, trailing curls of matching ribbon. She reached for one and drew it down, then caught another and another until she held an entire bouquet of vibrant colors.

"Careful or you'll float away," Frank teased from somewhere just beyond the balloons. He ducked beneath them to sit beside her. So it hadn't been a dream at all. He was here. She was glad enough to see him not to ask how he'd gotten in. She could guess anyway. Carolanne had the only other key to her apartment, and Carolanne thought she'd been wrong to cut herself off from Frank, from a chance at love.

"How do you feel, sleepyhead?" he asked.

"Better. What time is it?"

"Nearly eight. Are you hungry?"

"Starved, but there's nothing in the house for dinner."

He grinned. "Ah, but there is. Veal piccata, pasta and a chocolate mousse cake that will make you weep."

Her mouth watered at the tempting descriptions. "If you prepared all that, maybe we do have something to talk about after all."

"Meaning?"

"Meaning that I will reconsider on the spot marrying a man who can make a chocolate mousse cake."

Frank didn't seem especially pleased by the concession. Either he hadn't made the cake or she was missing something. "You're going to marry me, cake or no cake," he reminded her. "That's been decided."

Her gaze narrowed. "Since when?"

"Since three hours ago, when you swore to stop fighting me."

"I don't remember that conversation."

"Then let me remind you. You and me. Together, always. Those were the exact words."

"Yours or mine?"

"Mine, but you agreed. How can I take you on a honeymoon to Hawaii if you don't say yes?"

"Honeymoon?" she repeated weakly. "Did I agree to that, too? I must have been more out of it than I thought."

"Just sensible, for a change."

"Frank, I can't get married and I can't go to Hawaii. I have to wait here."

"For the test results," he said matter-of-factly. "No problem. They can call us in Hawaii. I hear the phone lines are very modern. No more tin cans or drums."

"No," she said, feeling the pressure build in her chest. "I will not marry you. Not until I know for sure."

He waved the tickets under her nose. "Nonrefundable. For tomorrow. We're going, Jenny Michaels, if I have to sling you across my shoulder and carry you onto that plane. You deserve a break, you need a rest and I'm going to see that you get it. If you want to wait to get married until after the honeymoon, that's a little weird, but it's something we can talk about."

She stared at him. "You want to take the honeymoon first?"

"I don't want to do it that way, but I'm willing to compromise. Just to prove what an agreeable sort of guy I am, what a catch."

She touched a hand to his cheek. "You are a catch. Any woman would be proud to marry you."

"I don't want any woman. I want you and I mean to have you."

"By bullying me into it?"

He grinned and taunted, "I learned from a master."

Jenny saw her own tactics coming back to haunt her. But even as she fought the idea of marrying Frank or even taking this idiotic trip he'd planned without consulting her, she couldn't deny that Hawaii with Frank sounded like heaven. Would it be selfish of her to go? Would it be cruel to start something they might not be able to finish?

As if he'd read her mind, Frank said, "We are going to live every single day as if it's the only one we've got. We are not going to put our lives on hold for 'what ifs.' I won't have either one of us waking up one day with regrets."

He kissed her then, stealing away her breath, teasing her senses until her spirits were soaring every bit as high as the balloons she'd allowed to drift away. "I'll go," she said, when she could finally catch her breath. It might be wrong, it might be selfish, but oh how she longed for a few more days of magic.

A triumphant smile broke across his rugged face. "The wedding?"

"One step at a time," she pleaded. "I can't take any more than that."

He nodded slowly. "One step at a time. We start with the honeymoon of a lifetime."

Less than twenty-four hours later they were on the beach in Maui where the breezes smelled of frangipani and the sun caressed almost as seductively as Frank. For three days they rested and swam and made sweet and tender love. There was no forbidden talk of the future, only the here and now and the delicious thrill of Frank's most persuasive touches, the joy of being together. Jenny felt healthier, more alive and more desperately in love than she ever had before.

On the fourth day when they came back to their cottage, the message light was blinking red. The sight of that impatient light was like a punch in her midsection. All of the energy and hope seemed to drain out of Jenny in the scant thirty seconds it took her to cross the room and call the desk.

As the operator read the name of her doctor and his number in San Francisco, Jenny reached instinctively for Frank's hand. Instead of taking her outstretched hand, though, he came up behind her and wrapped his arms around her waist. He pressed a kiss to the back of her neck, sending shivers down her spine, reminding her of all that was at stake. It was no longer simply her own existence that hung in the balance, but their future.

"I love you," he said urgently. "Marry me, Jenny. Say yes."

She turned in his arms and met his gaze. Her heart thundered in her chest, nearly breaking with despair. Oh, how she wanted to say yes, wanted to believe in the future, but she couldn't. It wouldn't be fair. "I can't answer you now," she said, but the words were an uncertain, breathless tremble.

He shook his head. "I want it settled before you make the call. I don't want there to be a single doubt that I'm asking because I love you or you're answering because of what's in your heart. Tell me now, Jenny. Do you love me?"

She wanted to do the right thing, the fair thing and deny it, but she couldn't. "More than life itself."

"Then that's our answer, isn't it?"

With a wobbly smile, she touched his lips. "Frank, are you sure? Really sure?"

"Absolutely. In sickness or in health."

She read the certainty in his eyes, heard the conviction in his voice, felt the love in his touch. "Then I guess that's our answer. I'll marry you."

Holding her tighter, giving her his strength, he said, "Now make the call."

When the nurse answered, Jenny had trouble even getting her name out. Her voice shook, but she took courage from Frank's embrace, from the commitment they had made only seconds before.

"Jenny," Dr. Hadley said in that low, soothing, bedside voice he had. "We have your results."

"And?"

"Everything looks good."

Hope, radiant and joyous, spilled over her like sunshine. "Everything?" she repeated.

"Not a sign of a recurrence. I'll want you in here a year from now, but I think there's every reason to be optimistic."

"Thank you," she whispered, her eyes locked with Frank's. Only one more year until that fateful fifth anniversary. One more. "You can't know how much this means to me."

"To both of us," Frank murmured huskily.

He took the phone from her grasp and replaced it in its cradle. With a sigh, he slanted his mouth over hers, filling her with an incredible sense of euphoria.

They had a chance, a real chance at a future, she thought as he tugged at the buttons on her beach coverup. When the gauzy material caught and tangled, he ripped it away with a fierce urgency that matched the rising tide of her own need. His hands were rough as he stripped her of her bathing suit, but the heated look in his eyes had her body shivering with the need for speed far more than finesse.

At the first daring touch of his tongue to her breast, excitement streaked through her like lightning. The last shred of self-consciousness between them shimmered, then disintegrated in a hot whirlwind of magical feelings. When he lifted his head to look in her eyes, cautiously seeking her reaction, she arched her back and drew him to her, wanting that exquisite, all-but-forgotten tug of need to go on forever. As pleasure built deep inside, she savored the bold strokes that told her again and again that she was woman enough for him. When his fingers sought the scar on her chest and his gaze locked with hers, she closed her hand over his and showed him the gentle caresses that inflamed and delighted.

There was no time to revel in each delicious sensation, because there were always more. Her body demanded and Frank gave, his lovemaking totally selfless. He reaffirmed the depth of his commitment again and again, building the aching hunger inside her.

With his kisses, slow, deep, passionate kisses that set her senses spinning.

With his caresses, the tenderest of touches, the boldest of claimings.

With his heart, his enduring love evident in his eyes, with the way he responded to her needs time and time again.

In moments, naked and filled with a wicked hunger, they tumbled together on the bed, a tangle of arms and legs, slick with perspiration, alive with desire.

"I love you," Frank said as he stilled above her, fulfillment an anxious heartbeat away. "I love you, Jenny."

"No more than I love you," she said fervently as their bodies at last joined together in a chaotic rhythm as old as time.

Never had Jenny been more aware of the rough and satin textures of his body, of the scent of saltwater and sweet air that surrounded them, of the way he tasted against her tongue or the way her body ached with need until the moment he slid inside her, making her whole, mending her dreams, reaffirming the sheer joy of living.

They were married on the beach a day later. She wore a white Hawaiian wedding dress, and he wore an impossibly loud shirt. She had a bright yellow flower tucked behind her ear and orchids for a bouquet. When they said their vows, Jenny stumbled over the words, but the commitment was etched forever in her heart.

When the brief ceremony was over and they were alone again, giddy on champagne and passion, Frank said, "You realize we're going to have to do this all over again in San Francisco?"

"Your family?"

"You bet. And it's our family now. Don't ever forget that."

"Don't you think with all those sons, your mother wouldn't mind missing this one wedding? My parents will be satisfied with a phone call."

"Not Ma. She'll be convinced we're living in sin unless she hears the vows for herself."

Jenny snuggled closer. "Could be fun," she teased. "It would add an element of danger, when things get too predictable."

"Things won't have a chance of getting predictable," Frank warned. "She's liable to move in with us until she's certain we've done the right thing."

"In that case, call ahead and line up the church. I am not going to give this up for a single night."

"I promise you, Jennifer Michaels Chambers, we will never be separated again. Never."

* * * * *

The spirit of motherhood is the spirit of love—and how better to capture that special feeling than in our short story collection...

Curtiss Ann Matlock
Carole Halston
Linda Shaw

to **Mother** *with* **Love** '92

Three glorious new stories that embody the very essence of family and romance are contained in this heartfelt tribute to Mother. Share in the joy by joining us and three of your favorite Silhouette authors for this celebration of motherhood and romance.

Available at your favorite retail outlet in May.

SILHOUETTE® Desire™

SILHOUETTE Desire 10TH Anniversary COLLECTION

Silhouette Desire 10th Anniversary

Celebrate with a FREE classic collection of romance!

In honor of its 10th Anniversary, Silhouette Desire has a gift for you! A limited-edition, hardcover anthology of three early Silhouette Desire titles, written by three of your favorite authors.

Diana Palmer   SEPTEMBER MORNING
Jennifer Greene   BODY AND SOUL
Lass Small   TO MEET AGAIN

This unique collection will not be sold in retail stores and is only available through this exclusive offer. Look for details in Silhouette Desire titles available in retail stores in June, July and August.

SDANN

FREE GIFT OFFER

To receive your free gift, send us the specified number of proofs-of-purchase from any specially marked Free Gift Offer Harlequin or Silhouette book with the Free Gift Certificate properly completed, plus a check or money order (do not send cash) to cover postage and handling payable to Harlequin/Silhouette Free Gift Promotion Offer. We will send you the specified gift.

FREE GIFT CERTIFICATE

ITEM	A. GOLD TONE EARRINGS	B. GOLD TONE BRACELET	C. GOLD TONE NECKLACE
# of proofs-of-purchase required	3	6	9
Postage and Handling	$1.75	$2.25	$2.75
Check one	☐	☐	☐

Name: _____

Address: _____

City: _____ State: _____ Zip Code: _____

Mail this certificate, specified number of proofs-of-purchase and a check or money order for postage and handling to: HARLEQUIN/SILHOUETTE FREE GIFT OFFER 1992, P.O. Box 9057, Buffalo, NY 14269-9057. Requests must be received by July 31, 1992.

PLUS—Every time you submit a completed certificate with the correct number of proofs-of-purchase, you are automatically entered in our MILLION DOLLAR SWEEPSTAKES! No purchase or obligation necessary to enter. See below for alternate means of entry and how to obtain complete sweepstakes rules.

MILLION DOLLAR SWEEPSTAKES
NO PURCHASE OR OBLIGATION NECESSARY TO ENTER

To enter, hand-print (mechanical reproductions are not acceptable) your name and address on a 3"×5" card and mail to Million Dollar Sweepstakes 6097, c/o either P.O. Box 9056, Buffalo, NY 14269-9056 or P.O. Box 621, Fort Erie, Ontario L2A 5X3. Limit: one entry per envelope. Entries must be sent via 1st-class mail. For eligibility, entries must be received no later than March 31, 1994. No liability is assumed for printing errors, lost, late or misdirected entries.

Sweepstakes is open to persons 18 years of age or older. All applicable laws and regulations apply. Sweepstakes offer void wherever prohibited by law. Prizewinners will be determined no later than May 1994. Chances of winning are determined by the number of entries distributed and received. For a copy of the Official Rules governing this sweepstakes offer, send a self-addressed, stamped envelope (WA residents need not affix return postage) to: Million Dollar Sweepstakes Rules, P.O. Box 4733, Blair, NE 68009.

✂ SD1U

ONE PROOF-OF-PURCHASE
To collect your fabulous FREE GIFT you must include the necessary FREE GIFT proofs-of-purchase with a properly completed offer certificate.

(See center insert for details)